COMPLETE

SATISFACTION

BRICKHOUSE

Phoenix Publishing House, LLC
Publishers since 2016

This novel is a work of fiction. Any references to real people, events, establishments, or locales are intended only to give the fiction a sense of reality or authenticity. Other names, characters, and incidents occurring in the work are either product of the author's imagination or are used fictitiously, as are those fictionalized events and incidents that involve real persons. Any character that happens to share the name of a person who is an acquaintance of the

Published by:
PHOENIX PUBLISHING HOUSE
P.O. BOX 154855
Lufkin, TX 75904

SYNOPSIS

Meet Ezrah King. He's a first responder turned police officer. It was a courageous move being that his father hates cops. He grew up in the civil rights era and is disgusted by his son's choice.

Although his friend Ivy Mitchell keeps blasting her shot louder than the Glock she carries on her hip, he doesn't know how many ways he can say he's not interested. His ex, Alysia, crawled into his life like unsuspecting cancer. From day one she manipulated her way to get close to him. His already paranoid nature was intensified by her deceitful act. He wasn't interested in trying his hand at love until Capria Malone.

Capria Malone is just your around the way girl trying her hardest to get up out of Greenspoint so she can live the life she knows she deserves. Her only problem is that she can't shake Pierre—a toxic boyfriend of seven years that's like a noose around her neck. She understands the need to let him go but doesn't want to feel like she wasted seven years of her life for nothing. Hanging on to Pierre is causing her to bleed out.

Can Ezrah be just the first responder she needs to resuscitate her back to life? Will Ivy just let Ezrah pursue the love that he wants, or will she suit up in her riot gear and go to war for what she wants?

PLEASE LEAVE A REVIEW WHEN YOU'RE DONE! I WOULD LOVE TO HEAR FROM YOU!

ACKNOWLEDGMENTS

Lord, I thank you for my gift of allowing me to write
and create stories that touch lives.

B.

CHAPTER ONE

CAPRIA

"Girl, I know you lyin'," I sigh through the phone to Lotti.

"Girl, what happened? Hello?"

"I think I've been robbed! My T.V. and DVD player is gone!"

"Oh my God! Is anything else out of place? Did they trash your apartment? You have some nice stuff in your apartment. Are you sure you were robbed?"

I know what Lottie is getting at. I told her I thought that Pierre was taking stuff from our apartment and pawning it a few days ago.

That's the only thing about telling people your business; they never miss the opportunity to throw it back in your face.

Pierre is always messing up and I always take him back. I've been with him for seven years and I just don't want all the pain and suffering to be in vain. I know that man better than anyone. All the good, bad, and ugly. I know he is capable of change and I want to be the woman by his side when he does.

I'm not about to mold him for some other chick to reap the benefits.

"Well, keep me posted. I have to go to therapy. And don't tell ya hatin' sister," she warns me before getting off the phone.

She was in therapy for something that happened at a trail ride awhile back.

Lottie and I were kickin' it at Lincoln City Park after a trail ride one Sunday. We should've been at church but the ride had been live all weekend, and we couldn't miss the close of it.

We were only at the park so we all could catch up. The horses also needed to rest a bit before we headed to the fairgrounds. That's where we would settle in for the night to dance and drink.

Leon Chavez's music was blaring through the speakers and some of the girls had started to dance and kick up dirt with their boots.

POP!

POP!

POP!

"Get down!" I yelled to Lottie.

The gunshots were so loud it startled the horses and got them riled up.

Lottie and I were sitting on top of her brother's money green Dually truck. He had 100-Spoke Straight Lace Chrome Rims to set it off and we were on top capping until everything hit the fan.

Self-perseveration kicked in and I fell down inside of the truck bed. I looked over and didn't see Lotti.

Once the smoke had cleared, I raised my head up out of the truck bed.

"Lotti! Lotti!" I screamed.

Tears started to fill my eyes when I didn't hear her respond.

I looked over the right side of the truck and didn't see anything.

People were running looking for their families and checking each other for bullet wounds.

"Lotti!" I called to her again looking over the left side of the truck. "Looottttiii!"
I jumped over the side once I spotted her.

She was lying on her stomach barely breathing. I could feel my muscles stiffen with the fear of losing my best friend.

It was a common thing here in the hood. I was tired of getting shirts made for people I was never meant to live without.

We had enough going on with the cops killing us.

I was only sure of one thing:. I wasn't losing Lotti! Not today...not ever!

People started to crowd around us. My hands trembled so bad I could barely keep them steady as I felt for a pulse.

I placed my hand over my back pocket where my phone was, but it was gone.

"Don't nobody touch her and call 9-1-1! She's been shot!" I swung my body around towards the crowd of people.

Once I was leaning over my best friend I could see more blood starting to soak through her clothes. My breath snagged hold on to the fear inside my chest.

I took the flannel shirt I had wrapped around my waist to cover Lotti's butt. She had pissed her pants. I wasn't about to have my girl out here exposed on social media.

"Stop filming her! Who raised you trash bums!" I yelled!

"Yo, put them phones down!" Lil' Marco from seven ninety, that's what we called Lincoln City Apartments, brandished his semi-automatic as he addressed the crowd.

Lotti was his sister and I was sure those shots had something to do with him.

Lil' Marco had paid his dues in the streets. Anyone running up on him understood fully what came with his level of crazy.

Marco left a trail of bodies he never went down for. We knew when we rolled with him our life was on the line.

But who thinks they're going to die? Really.

Everyone did as he asked. He couldn't even kneel down to check on Lotti for trying to watch his back.

It was cool, I had her.

"Pria, you have to stay with her. I can't be here when they get here, but I'll meet y'all at the hospital."

"Marco, don't you dare leave us here! This is your sister!" I shot him a venomous look.

He held my gaze for a moment before looking away without a word. He wasn't going to stay with us.

I was terrified. We still don't know who let out the shots or if they were still there waiting to pop us again.

"Man, stop being soft! You know what a nigga dealin' with. Yo, I gotta go!"

And just like that, people made space so he could pull his truck out.

Thankfully Lotti had fallen a few feet from the top of the truck. That negro probably would've run one of her legs over to protect his freedom.

I couldn't get mad at Marco because we all understood how he was, but this was his sister!

"Hang on, Lotti! Hang on, baby! I'm here!"

I was no longer paying attention to anything other than keeping my best friend alive.

I couldn't count on my sister to do anything but drag my name through the dirt, so Lotti was all I had .

This was the scariest day of my life. As promised, Lil' Marco met us at the hospital. The bullet had grazed her spine.

The waiting room was littered with people from the trail ride. Most were being nosey others were pouring in from minor injuries from the incident at the park.

I was dazed staring at the poster on the wall advocating for the onlooker to opt for telemedicine rather than bombarding the emergency room with frivolous visits.

The lady at the desk registering her daughter was pressing down so hard with the pen you could hear the scratching of it as she signed the forms.

"Initial here, here, here, and here to give consent for the doctor to treat her today," she instructed.

The ragged torn seat cushioning was tearing at the back of my leg making my wait more irritable.

I snatched glances at other patients in the waiting room and couldn't help but wonder why they were here.

Marco was on his phone most likely trying to find out who the shooter was.

With every passing hour, the waiting room began to thin out with visitors. It was almost eight o'clock at night and the fairgrounds were about to get lit.

People weren't about to miss that move so they bounced with the quickness.

"Are you the family of Lotisha Caney?" the doctor asked.

"Yeah, that's my sister," Marco's raspy voice responded.

His voice sounded as if he smoked cigarettes all his life because he did.

"The bullet grazed her spine causing it to swell. She's paralyzed, but we're not sure if it's permanent or not. Once she's out of recovery and in her room we'll let you both in to see her. It'll be a few hours, so if you want to leave and come back you can," he instructed us both.

"Aight. Bet," Marco said. *"You need a ride?"* he asked.

"I'm not leaving. I'll stay here and wait for her to be put in her room."

"Okay, just hit my phone with the room number. I'll bring you something to eat back."

"I'm not hungry," I declined his offer.

"I know you worried about Lotti, but you need to put something on your stomach. I'm not asking you! I'm telling you I'm bringing you something back. You need anything else between time just text me."

It was only a couple of hours before the nurse came and got me to bring me up to Lotti's room.

She was still sleeping when I walked in.

I took a seat in the well-worn visitor chair. I fumbled around with it until I found out how to adjust it into a mini bed. I refused to leave her side until she was awake.

Once she realized that she couldn't move her legs, I knew she was going to freak out.

The dingy towels were placed on the window seal along with some pillowcases.

"Hey Pria," Lotti choked out.

"Hey, try not to move. Let me get your nurse," I instructed her.

I hurried and pressed the red button to call her nurse before she noticed the lack of movement in her legs and freaked out with just us in here.

"I can't feel my legs!" she screamed. "What's wrong with my legs, Pria?"

Her words sent chills down my spine. How could I tell my best friend she had one of the hardest roads we had yet to journey down together?

"Calm down, boo. I got you," I pleaded with her. "The bullet grazed your spine. The doctor said it just may be temporary, but it's a waiting game."

"So, you 're telling me I gotta wear diapers and wait for somebody to help me do what I need to do?"

It broke my heart to watch the tears pour from my friend's eyes.

Both of our hearts were breaking. Lotti was a go-getter and didn't ask anyone for anything. Not even her brother Marco.

I held her close as we waited for the nurse to come in and confirm what I just told her.

Lord, give my baby strength. I silently prayed.

*   *   *

Lotti never misses therapy and she's constantly trying to lift herself out of that chair despite her doctor warning her to take it slow.

She has her own mind though. Once she has it set on something, it's a done deal.

It's only been about six months since the shooting, but she's getting antsy.

I always come with her for support and to make sure she listens to her physical therapist.

Her hour-long session is just about over, and we're just waiting for Marco to pull up.

"How did she do today?" he asks, sneaking up on me.

"Boy, you scared me!" I snap.

"I told you about not watchin' yo' back. I don't care if you at this fancy place. You need to be on point at all times, ma'," he scolds me.

After Lotti's shooting, he's on us more than ever about watching our surroundings even though it's his fault she got shot in the first place.

He'll never admit to it, but we all know what's up.

"I'm almost ready, bro." Lotti smiles as the therapist positions her back in her chair.

"Take ya' time."

Once she's settled, she hit the switch on her wheelchair towards me and Marco.

"Let's blow this joint," she demands.

Marco lifts her out of the chair and sits her in the back seat of the truck. He puts her chair on the back. I watch his muscles flex as he struggles to lift the heavy chair.

Man, that chair weighs a ton, so I have no idea how he does it.

Meg the Stallion's song *Savage* blares through the speakers. The bass forces the dashboard to tremble.

I hate how loud he blasts his music. Lotti is in the back bobbin' her head looking out the window.

I wonder what is going through her mind.

Forty-five North is clear for the most part so we make it to our apartment complex within thirty minutes.

"Aight, y'all. Lotti, call me when you get settled." I blow her a kiss as I head into my apartment.

I walk into the bedroom to see if Pierre has taken anything. It's now a part of my routine when I enter my apartment.

Pierre, you mutha...

Pierre works, but all of it isn't making its way to our apartment.

"Aaagghh!" I scream at the top of my lungs when I notice the mouse shoot under the door of my bedroom closet. "I hate it here!"

If it isn't one thing, it's another here in Coppertree Village. There is always a fight or shoot out in this death trap. If the hood didn't get you, the bed bugs will eventually eat you out of here.

A lady in the next building had to cut all her hair off just to get rid of the ones she had. She's a thot too, so we're not sure what she has going on.

I jump off my bed even more pissed at Pierre. He should be home from work by now. He's supposed to put the rat traps out two days ago!

He can chase some cat but can't take care of home. I'm getting sick of him.

Who am I kidding? I love the hell out of him. People don't know the real reason I can't shake him. I can't do better than Pierre.

CHAPTER TWO

EZRAH

I'm shielding my sister in the bathtub as .50 caliber bullets echo through the streets. The death of Botham Jean sent the city up. Another senseless killing of an unarmed African American released a rage that our ancestors echoed. It happened in Dallas, which made it too close for comfort for those of us who live in Houston.

"I think they stopped," Meme whispers like we're under direct assault.

"I think you're right."

We climb out of the tub and I make my way to my bedroom. I just graduated with my degree in Criminal Justice and have been accepted into the police academy.

The letter weighed a ton in my hands. I have to tell my dad, who is a prominent civil rights leader in Houston, that I'm becoming something he despises. He's been very vocal during the Black Lives Matter Movement. The last thing he's going to do is accept me wanting to become a cop.

My father grew up in the sixties, so this is like déjà vu to him. The police harassment, stereotypes, and assault on people of color for no reason.

"You know you're going to have to tell him before you leave for the academy this weekend."

"I know. He's going to hit the roof, Meme, and you know it."

"He'll be alright. You know I got your back. I understand why you're doing this. You just make sure you don't conform to their ways. Be the change that our people need on the force. Represent us with integrity."

"I will do my best to."

"No, do it."

"I hear you, baby sister."

In eighteen weeks, I will be done with my training.

I remember the first time I heard the .50 caliber bullets rain down in the city about a year ago. The next day I stepped over the rubble to get to the corner store. When I came out of the house, cops were parked outside near the curb putting the gun away.

"How fast does it go?"

The cop closest to me pointed a nickel-plated pistol in my face and said, "It goes fast. Now get away from the car!"

In that moment, a year ago, of being over-policed and treated like nothing, I knew I had to be the change in my community.

I'm signing up to police my neighborhood and keep it safe. Despite what my dad thinks, I know what I'm doing is honorable. I've been toiling over my decision for a year and I know now is the right time.

I'm grateful that sleep started to set in. My eyelids became just as heavy as my heart. In the morning, I have to face my dad.

*   *   *

I feel around for my phone on the nightstand. My alarm is going off and it's doing its job. The rooster crowing is belting through the speakers.

"Shut that thing up!"

Meme isn't a morning person at all.

"You have to get up for class anyway! Hush up, girl!"

It makes sense for us to be roommates. I haven't been with anyone since Alysia, so females aren't running through here.

Meme knows better than to bring anyone around that she isn't serious about. Me and my dad are at a man's neck if he tries to be in her life.

"Are you telling Daddy today?"

"Yeah."

"You nervous?"

"Of course, I am. Daddy hate cops with a passion after how they did him back in the day. The beatings, pepper spray, dog attacks, water hoses, and the list goes on of what they experienced while protesting. That mistreatment left a stain on his soul, Meme, and you know it."

"Nevertheless, you might as well get it over with. Who knows, maybe he will understand."

I take my time getting dressed. I feel like rocks are piling up in my stomach. I'm thirty-two and it's time I start living for myself.

I've enjoyed being a First Responder, but I'm tired of getting to the scene just in time to clean up the chaos. I want to try and prevent bad things from happening to good people. That's another reason it's taken me so long to switch over. I still love what I did. I know a few people on the force. One is my homegirl Ivy. Our paths cross so much, we eventually became friends. She flirts with me, but I'm not interested in her like that. I mean, she's fine, but after Alysia I've just been on chill mode.

The tires moan against the street as I make my drive to my dad's house. I make a left on Ella Drive and pull in front of my dad's house.

When he retired from the oil field, he wanted to stay in the hood, so he just had his house rebuilt on his property. The white ranch style house adorns black shutters. The bushes in front of his house are neatly trimmed. The smell of fresh grass irritates my sinuses, sending me into a sneezing spell.

My daddy has his black barrel pit going. I can smell the apple wood entwined with the coals. It's Friday, and I'm leaving tomorrow which left little time for him to badger me.

My dad is hard but fair. He cares about me but only shows affection to my sister. He's always told me I have to be tough as a man in this world if I want to survive and thrive.

I personally didn't feel like a bit of affection from my father would turn me soft like the Pillsbury Dough Boy.

"What you doin' at my house this early?"

"I wanted to stop by and talk to you about something, Daddy."

"And what's that?"

He flips his ribs before walking back inside.

He heads into the kitchen which is my cue to follow him.

He begins mixing up his infamous barbecue sauce while he sipped on his Budweiser.

"Dad, I leave for the police academy tomorrow."

I stand there waiting for him to blow his top.

"You come up in my house to tell me that you are about to become a traitor? You think them white cops on that force gon' look out for your black tail? If they don't get you the streets will! You know how many crazy fools out here killing folks for no reason? Ezrah, you are the only son I got! You'll never succeed on that force because you ain't gon' be nothin' but another nigga to them! Your mama would roll over in her grave if she knew you were about to do this!"

"Mama would be proud of me. Just like she was when she found out I was going to be a first responder. Dad, I'm a grown man. I don't need your permission or approval, but I wanted you to know. I want to be the change not just talk about the change in the community. We need more faces that look like us out there policing our hoods."

"Well when you get there, see if you can get the ones already in there to stand up for their people. Help them join you in this supposed change. You know how I feel about cops, and I will feel the same about you in that uniform. Now get out of my house."

I drop my head in defeat. I'mdelusional thinking I can get an inkling of support from my father.

My mind is made up and I'm not changing it for anyone. I have to be true to my own convictions. My father has rejected me all my life so this wouldn't be anything different.

I'm glad I have to volunteer at the community center today. Playing basketball with underprivileged teenage boys is the highlight of my week.

Most of them don't have their fathers in their lives, so I try to teach them the things my dad taught me. He's never hugged me, but he made sure I know everything there is about being a man.

"Hey, Tina! My boys in there already?"

"You know they waitin' to clown you on that court," she laughs.

Tina is the facility director at the community center. She's always thinking of creative things to do and bring to the kids.

"Cody. Let me holla at you for a minute." I wave him over to me.

Cody has been coming to the community center for about a month. His mother is a single parent so she works a lot. Even with all the hours she puts in at the hospital it's just not enough to take complete care of a teenage son. Cody is already six feet tall and he's only fifteen.

"What's up, Coach?"

"Where your backpack?"

"Over there?"

"Go and grab it for me real quick."

He jogs over and did as I asked.

"I got you these." I pull the Air Maxes out of my duffle bag and hand them to him.

"I can't take those, Coach." He backs up against the wall.

"Why not?"

"I don't know. Ain't nobody ever gave me nothin'."

"Well, there's a first time for everything."

"What I gotta do?"

"You ain't gotta do nothin'."

"For real?"

"For real. I had you bring your bag over here so people won't be all up in our business. Make sure you take your bag to Ms. Tina. She will make sure nobody steals your shoes."

"Thank you, Coach." He towers over me as he holds me in a bear hug.

This is why I do what I do.

"Cody, put my card in your bag just in case your mama want to call and ask me anything about the shoes."

"Alright, Coach."

Cody isn't the only one I've bought shoes for. I've done things for all my boys and will continue to. As long as they're trying, I'm going to do everything in my power to keep them on the right path.

CHAPTER THREE

NAY-NAY

"Man, you said I could come by and nibble on you so stop playin' with me, Nay," Pierre begs.

Pierre has his thirsty butt over here trying to eat on some cat. I'm about to let him after he begs a lil' more.

I have a blunt in one hand with my legs spread. My cat is sitting up in my black panties, and Pierre is biting on his bottom lip.

Pierre is a dark chocolate sexy something. Half of Acres Home wants that broke demon pipe between his legs. He has the whitest teeth and waves deep enough to drown your soul.

His tongue is long and his pipe is longer. He has my sister Pria sprung. After months of telling her he ain't nothin' but a dog and her not listening, I've decided she needs to learn the hard way.

I had every intention of exposing him, but that rod is to bomb. I cann't just walk away from it without a few more interactions.

All of Acres Home knows he out here screwin' like a rabbit, and he for the streets.

The only smart thing my sister did do was not get pregnant by him.

I plan on popping him out one if he keeps laying pipe the way he is. That is a guarantee that I will always have access to him.

I exhale the smoke in his face and push him headfirst between my legs.

My kids arere at school, but it isn't uncommon for Uncle Pierre to be over. They assume we're in the room getting high.

I don't feel bad about anything I'm doing. If Monique wants to be dumb that's on her. She needs to be brought down a peg or two anyway.

We all stay in the hood. Ain't one person better than the other! I stay in the back of the apartment building and Monique lives in the front. I'm never worried about her catching him over here because we never talk. Besides, she knows better than to pop up at my crib.

We aren't beefing but we just don't mess with each other like that.

Hell, everybody in the hood knows that we're freakin'. He's high off the vibe of screwin' two sisters.

"Girl, you gon' get me in trouble," Pierre pants as he releases his kids on my stomach.

I take my finger and swirl a circle around my belly button.

"Freak." He smiles.

"For you." I smile seductively.

"Nay. I have to get home. I'm already late." He pulls away as I lock him between my legs.

"I thought you had some money for me?" I whine. "I need to keep these pre-paid lights on. I only have about six dollars left on there."

"I told you I got you."

He pulls out sixty dollars and hands it to me.

"I have to go. I'll be by tomorrow after work."

"Nah, I got my baby daddy coming over to give me some more money," I tell him.

"Let that nigga be here when I get off, Nay, and I'm gon' drag both of y'all, on my mama!"

"Boy, you live with my sister. This is not yours!" I slap my hand against my cat. "I just bust you down from time to time."

Pierre slams the door shut and rushes towards me.

WAP!

"Stop playing with me, Nay. Just because I'm on probation don't get it twisted! I'm still the nigga in these streets!"

I hold the side of my face. I don't know why, but it turns me on when he hits me. It lets me know that he cares about me.

Pierre was on before he got locked up, but that nigga still ain't back on. Always talkin' about what he used to have.

"Alright, P!"

"Come here!"

Holding my face, I did as he asked.

He snakes his tongue down my throat while holding a firm grip on it.

How did wanting some pipe with a bit of complication get me here?

CHAPTER FOUR

CAPRIA

"Where in the hell have you been?" I snatch the door open before Pierre could get it open with his key.

He walks past me as if I haven't said anything. His level of disrespect has me about to show him a side of me he's never seen.

"You probably been somewhere laid up!" I stand in his path blocking him. "Where is my T.V. and DVD player?"

"I needed some money for something," is all he said.

He doesn't care about takin' from me. That's all he does is take, take, take, and I'm starting to get tired.

He's taking it too far.

"You needed it for what? That was the only thing I was able to get myself when I got my taxes back!"

"Look, a nigga gon' give that lil' money back to you!"

"Give it back to me? I want my electronics back! It cost way more than whatever you pawned it for! You are acting real hypish right now! For real!"

"Who is you talkin' to? I will rock ya' right now. Stop playing with me." He pushes his finger into the center of my forehead.

"It's not going to be fun when the rabbit gets the gun, P." I turn and head to the room in tears.

After about thirty minutes, P came in the room.

"Baby, a nigga ain't used to a nine to five. Hustlin' is all I know. That was always how I took care of myself. I know I should've listened when you was tellin' me to stack that bread. I was out here tryna stunt on these niggas. I wasn't thinking about eating in the long run. Nigga thought he was gon' always be on. I'm not cheatin', but a nigga tryna just survive the next couple of months left on paper."

His eyes are sincere, and I believe him. I always believe him.

Pierre has been working at a factory over in the Heights that isn't paying nowhere near what he'sused to making selling drugs.

I made him promise to go legit when he got out. I'm not sure how long he will last, but I doubt we'll together much longer the way things are headed.

"My dad is coming by tomorrow to drop off some barbecue. He's grilling tonight. I know we both got to work so I told him we couldn't stop by tonight."

"Okay," is all I said.

Pierre came and nestles next to me. His attempt to solve problems involved sex. I love making love to him so I'm cool with it.

He didn't even bother to get fully undressed so I know what this is. A quickie to shut me up.

"Why yo' cat loose?" he asks mid stroke.

"What the hell you mean? My cat not loose, the hell wrong with you?"

"I mean, I can feel everything, but...are you smashin' somebody else, Pria?"

"Are you serious right now? You know better than that! I can't believe you fixed your mouth to talk down on me, nigga!"

"Maybe it's from you working out all the time. I told you to stop a long time ago. Who are you trying to stay fit for anyway? I'm just saying, other chicks work out all the time and they cat still wrap."

"They cat still wrap? You're sitting here comparing me to some slut you done screwed, my nigga?"

I'm fuming. How dare he!

"Stop being so defensive. Why don't you do some of those Kegel exercises or something? I heard that keep women twat tight."

"You sure educated on cat all of a sudden. You never complained before, now it's a problem. You blessed I let you between my legs. I ain't doin' jack!"

I grab my robe and wrap it around me and went into the living room.

I've never felt so humiliated and inadequate.

Pierre and I have been drifting apart for some time. If he is cheating, I've never caught him or found anything. I've never really looked either.

My mom always says, "If you go looking for something, you'll find it."

I've never looked because I'm afraid of what I will find and maybe I won't have the strength to leave.

I pop Baby Boy in and watch it until my eyes became heavy.

My pussy is magical! I don't know what he talmbout!

***

"Wake up!" Lotti yells in the phone once I answer it.

I'm surprised that Pierre is already gone for work.

"You know I hate you waking me up before I have to be at work. I need all my sleep!" I whine, sitting up on the edge of the bed.

"Why is Pierre going in Nay apartment this early in the morning? You sent him over there?"

"What you are doing in the back of the apartments?"

"Don't worry about all that! Why is your man at your sister's who you don't mess with 'cause she's triflin' house?"

"I don't know, but I'm about to find out!"

"Don't be stupid and call. Pop the hell up if you wanna know what's trill!"

She was right, but I'm not prepared for what I may find.

I head to the bathroom to empty my gut. My stomach is in knots I'm so nervous.

I put on my shorts, t-shirt, and Air Maxes and book it around to the back.

I cover the peephole with my hand and beat on the door.

"Office!" I yell, disguising my voice.

"I told y'all I was going to pay it on the tenth!" my sister Nay yells.

She stays on her back but can't pay a bill to save her life.

I continue to beat on the door until she finally swings it open.

"I…be…," I say, barely above a whisper.

Pierre is lounging back on the couch naked. His meat is so hard it is protruding from under the towel she must've thrown over him in a hurry.

"You dirty-!" I yell, grabbing Nay by her hair.

I'm the oldest, so beating her down is nothing new.

At first, Pierre didn't even move! He just laughs until I grab the stone ashtray from her table.

"Pria, no!" He snatches it from my hand.

I get up off my sister and throw the folding chair in the dining room at him, gashing his head open.

He doesn't like that at all.

"Go home!"

"You triflin'! We both about to be for the streets, my nigga. My sister though, P? Out of all the women…you chose my sister? You know she hates me and prays on my downfall! I've been nothing but loyal and faithful to you! You can have her! She can't even keep her child alive."

"I'll kill you! Don't speak on my son! Let me go!" she screams as she fights to break free from Pierre.

"Let her go so I can break her down some more," I challenge him.

"Just go home!"

When I walk out, we've woken up the entire apartment complex, and it'ss evident by the crowd holding their phones recording.

"Girl, they been messin' around!" someone in the crowd yells.

I lower my head in shame as I make my way back to my end of the apartment complex.

Of all people, he chooses my sister. Got me out here looking stupid in front of all these people. I'm humiliated. I'm so mad, I feel as if fifty daggers are being lunged at my back all at once.

I refuse to let these people see me cry.

I pull out my vibrating phone. Pierre's father is texting saying he'sfive minutes away.

Wait until I tell him about his slime ball son!

I wait on the stairs for Polo. We call him that because it's all he wears other than the western wear for trail rides.

Pierre didn't bother coming after me. I bet he's still over there laying pipe to my sister. I should go and shoot her spot up. My nephews are at school anyway.

Polo pulled up. "What's wrong with you?"

"Nothing," I respond barely above a whisper.

"Don't let my son get you down. Let me park—we gon' eat and drink some Hennessy."

He says rather than asks.

I head back into my apartment and sit on the couch.

I feel like less than nothing from actions that aren't my own. I'm not going to school today. There's no way I will be able to concentrate anyway.

Polo has come over plenty of times, so he makes himself at home in the kitchen.

He ignores the roaches and rinses our cups out.

"Here, drink this." He shoves the cup in my face.

I gulp it down without hesitation. Anger spirals from the pit of my stomach. I toss around the idea of going back to Nay's house to beat down on her again.

"Let me tell you something about my son. If you let him run you over, he will do just that. He will run anyone down for what he wants." He takes another drink as if more is behind his comment.

The longer it took Pierre to come home, the more I drank. I really want Polo to leave so I can go for another round.

"I'm not leaving until you calm down. Don't go back around that corner showing out in front of them people who don't care nothing about you. He wanna lay up over there, then tell him to move in with her. Put yo' foot down!"

Tears fill my eyes. I'm tired of crying and playing it safe.

Polo has always been sexy, and I admire how he is oblivious to the fact that he still has it going on. He is an older version of Pierre but he's settled. Ever since Pierre's mother passed, he just keeps to himself.

He pours all his love into his children without wavering, despite the bums they are.

I scoot closer to Polo, and he doesn't budge. I wonder if he can take away my heartache in another way.

I don't know if it was because he's forbidden or if I'm thirsty for revenge; either way, my panties are soaked. I'm about to make Pierre my stepson.

"Alright, nah, I ain't my son. I'll break ya' little tail off!"

I'm shocked by his response. He's never really spoken to me like that before.

"I really just need to feel something else besides the pain I'm feeling."

Without saying a word, he got up and bolted the door. Even if P tries to come home, I won't let him in.

Polo takes me by the hand and stands me up in front of him. He kisses me gently before picking me up and securing my legs around his waist.

It's been years since I've slept with another man, and despite my motive, I want Polo savagely in this moment.

After hours of him doing things to my body that I've never known were possible, he brings me a towel from the bathroom so I can wash up.

"Are you hungry? I still have that barbecue in there. I can warm it up for us. Let's put a movie on and watch it while we eat." He smiles.

"I would love that." I smile.

Instead of using the washcloth, I got in the shower while he made us something to eat.

Half-way through the movie and our food, I can hear footsteps coming up the concrete path.

"Yo, why the fuck the bolt on the door?" P yells from the other side.

"Cause ya don't live here no more!" I yell back.

His father gently places his hand on his knee. "Let him in and talk like adults," he whispers.

I look at him and did as he requests.

"Why y'all in here with the door locked?"

"Pierre don't play with me. Respect me before I break ya' fragile frame down, son."

Pierre fell in line. He may have these niggas thinking he was some type of savage, but he knows his dad will shoot him and drive him to the hospital.

Polo has his conceal and carry license so he stays with his gun on his hip.

"My bad, Daddy. She just on some B.S. right now."

"I'm on B.S.? You're screwing my sister and stayed apparently until you finished! You can get your stuff and move in with her."

"I'm glad we on the same page," he spit.

I want to take the Hennessy bottle and bust his head open to the white meat!

He's so bold with it. He really doesn't care after all that I've done for him!

I look over at his dad who throws both of his hands up, gesturing that he isn't in what we have going on.

I refuse to give Pierre any more than I've given him. Besides, his daddy lays better pipe anyway.

*   *   *

Pierre left the rest of that Hennessy for me last night, and I've made an attempt to find the solution to my problems at the very bottom.

I can't believe the blatant disrespect last night from them.

I roll over to grab my phone, hoping Pierre will be begging to come home.

I have over ten missed calls from my mother, but that's it.

I know she's calling because she heard about us fighting.

After my morning poop, I'll call her.

Our conversation will be filled with her telling me that I'm the oldest and blah, blah, blah.

She's always making excuses for Nay, and I'm tired of hearing them.

I make sure I have everything in my backpack. I'm almost done with my classes to become an esthetician.

I send a confirmation text to my client. I'm so ready to apply everything I've been learning. I've started booking clients and turned one of my bedrooms into a mini spa.

I push the door open to expose the powder pink walls. I have oversized flowers the same color with black ones to accent.

I plant my feet in the furry pink area rug. I make my own seat for my Yoni Steams. Just because I'm providing a spa experience from my home doesn't mean it has to be ghetto.

With Pierre gone, I can now focus on my business and leveling up.

I pull the door closed and head out. As soon as I step out, Pierre and Nay Nay are purposely strolling by my apartment.

Their hands are entwined, and I cringe watching her plant her full crusty lips on him.

My stomach is throwing a kickboxing match.

Don't go to jail. Don't go to jail.

I remind myself they aren't worth the energy as I walk past them.

I refuse to give them the satisfaction of seeing me squirm.

"Heeeeyyy, sis," Nay Nay teases.

"Girl, go find you somebody to play with before I snatch the rest of your struggling edges bald."

"Is you mad or naw?" she cackles.

"Girl, I ain't bothered by you takin' out my trash," I spit, pushing past them.

I'm more determined than ever to push through. This come up is about to be something crucial. As soon as I stack enough money, I'm moving.

I dip behind my building and follow the cobblestone path to my sister's apartment. She never locks her door because she's always too high to keep up with her keys.

It's early so no one is outside but the crackheads. I hurry up my sister's stairs and go inside her apartment. It smells like rotten fish. She never cleans up and it is beyond me how any man can lay up in a filthy house.

I personally would feel like the cat ain't clean.

I go in her bathroom and grab her Nair off the shelf. I go into her bedroom and squeeze it in her Motions shampoo she keeps on her dresser.

She hates when my nephews mess with her stuff so she keeps her good stuff in her room.

Nay Nay only wants P because he was mine, and once P realizes that all she has to offer is between her legs, he will bore quickly and cheat on her too.

I put everything back the way it was and bounce to the bus stop.

"Heeeyyy!" I called out to the bus driver.

He slammed on his brakes and waits for me.

"I was wondering if you were going to school today," Mr. Luther says.

He's a bald bus driver with a goatee. His blue uniform is always neatly pressed and his socks are always gleaming white.

"Yes, sir. You know I ain't missin' no school."

"You better not." He waves his finger at me.

I smile and make my way to my seat. I can tell the other people on the bus are irritated but I didn't care. I'm tired of people. But mostly, I'mtired of myself and what I have allowed to unfold in my life.

The bus drops me off right in front of the school. I'malready starting to feel better. When I'mat school, nothing else matters. I'm in my happy place.

"Hey, boo!" Meredith runs up and hugs me.

I call her Meme for short.

She's my motivation. Well, we push each other.

"My first client is meeting me when I get off work." I break out in the Tootsie Roll.

"You better work, girl!"

Meme and I always partner up so our instructor don't bother asking who we're working with.

Class goes by fast as usual and I hate for it to end.

"Did that lady with the Nestle Crunch face tip you?" Meredith asks.

"Girl, nope! Just triflin' doin' all that complaining about a ten-dollar facial and still didn't tip after I had that skin glowing like a Sunkist orange."

"Don't trip. Pretty soon, we gon' be in our own shop checkin' a bag."

"Already."

"I can drop you off if you want."

"Thanks, boo. I appreciate it. I need to find me another crib. I'm not about to be around with Pierre and my sister."

"What do you mean, Pierre and your sister?"

My glare falls to the floor so Meme can't see my tears. I'm acting like it doesn't matter, but deep inside, it's tearing me up that my sister is running around with my man.

"Yep, just found about them the other day. You know she's always been jealous of me. Everything that I've ever had, she's wanted. I'm just trying to get my money together, Meme, so I can move to the other side of Houston."

"Come be my roommate! You know I have that extra room now that my brother is away."

"Thank you, but I have to do this on my own. Besides, I turned my other room to a mini spa."

"I'm not ready for all of that yet, but you ain't playin'!"

"You know we tryna get this schmoney. I don't have to wait for a shop. I can use what I have now to start our foundation."

I pull my planner out of my bag.

"What you about to do?" she asks.

"I'm making a to-do list for this week. We're going to design our business cards, get a website, and create business pages on social media."

"You are really serious, huh?"

"My life depends on this. I know I'm supposed to be living a certain way, and it's starting to bother me mentally, physically, and emotionally that I'm not. I know I can do better, so I'm going to bust my butt to do just that."

I look down at my phone.

"Is that him?" Meme asks.

"No, my client."

"What she say?"

"Girl, listen to this."

I just Googled the address, and it's at an apartment complex. I didn't know that or I wouldn't have booked with you. You should let people know that up front. It's not professional doing people's faces in the kitchen. Every experience I've had with someone doing business out their house has been horrible. I'm going to have to cancel.

"Girl, forget that bald-headed gutter snipe!"

Meme is hot about what my client texted. I guess she isn't my client since she cancelled.

"And tell her when she circles back it's going to cost double," she continues. "Girl, your people really be blowing me!"

"I just texted her that it's not in my kitchen, but I understand her concerns and thanked her for considering me."

"Girl, you better than me."

"I'm serious about building my brand. The last thing I need is for her to post these messages and it'll be my luck they go viral."

"Viral or not, she wouldn't be playing with me like that."

"Girl, why she still textin' me?"

"I mean at this point, what else does she have to say? She expressed her shade. You responded classy like and kept it moving. What does she want?"

"Talking about I really need to not book people until I'm in my shop and no one's going to book facials to sit in someone's kitchen."

"Give me that phone!"

Meme swerves the car trying to get my phone from me.

"No, Meme. It's not worth it."

The messages keep coming through, but I'm over it.

"After I graduate, I'm going to start my certifications to become a Crime Scene Cleaner."

"What? Why?"

"I've already linked with a company that's paying for my certifications. I'm so excited, so I need you to support me on this."

"Meme, do you know how dangerous that is? You run the risk of coming in contact with bloodborne pathogens and risk other health issues dealing with people's bodily fluids."

"I thought about all that, but I'll be safe. I promise! I just want to bring healing to these families who experience loss. I mean they all won't be gruesome crime scenes. People die from natural causes too, Pria. It's draining for a family to have to do that. I want to take that weight off them, Pria. I can do this. I haven't told my brother either."

"We've been in school for six months, and I still haven't met him."

"Girl, ain't nothin' special about Ezrah."

"Well, thanks, boo!" I hug Meme before I get out.

"If you need a ride anywhere make sure you call me. You want to spend the weekend with me? We can look at some apartments and watch Netflix while eating our favorite snacks."

"Sounds good."

CHAPTER FIVE

LOTTI

I watch Pria get out the car with Meme. She's some girl that she's been hanging out with at school. I've told her about having other friends, but she just won't listen.

When the car pulls out of the parking lot, I wheel to my door onto the porch.

"Hey, school slut." I laugh.

"Yeah, okay. What you got goin' on?" She tosses her book bag over her shoulder.

"Nothing. Same ole' same. Your sister and ex been parading around all day looking like they stink."

"I don't want to hear about them. I'm moving on, and I don't want to hear any negativity."

"Excuse me. What you are doing this weekend?"

"Going over to Meme's place," she says.

"What you about to do over there?"

"Plan some stuff out for my business and just chill. You know I don't do the club scene."

"You don't even know that girl like that to be spending the night at her house. You be too friendly out here in these streets. That's why you always end up looking stupid. Why don't you chill with me instead?"

"Nah, I'm good."

"You good? Aight, bet."

"You really changed since the accident, Lotti."

"If you got shot and ended up paralyzed, then you would change, too! It ain't all sunshine and roses over here. You know what it's like trying to get on the toilet and piss yourself before you can get your pants down? Yeah, I didn't think so! Go hang out with your new friend, but don't come crawling back over here when she crosses you!"

"All this because I wouldn't cancel my plans to hang around here with you. You think I want to see them walking past my house everyday being messy? I'm trying to hustle so I can get up out of here. As a friend you should understand that like I understand you're a jerk sometimes, because you're trying to cope with life."

"Whatever." I wheel myself back in the house, leaving her on the porch.

I secretly envy and resent her all at the same time. She's pressing forward in life and I'm stuck in this chair.

I pull out my blunt and light the end. The only thing good about being in this chair is the medical weed. It's stronger than anything floating around on the street.

"Are you kiddin' me?" I watch CAPRIA run back out of her apartment.

I saw Pierre and her sister go in there earlier, but that isn't my business. Since she wants to act brand new, I feel she needs a reminder of who really has her back.

"Lotti!" she screams, beating my door down.

"What?" I snatch it open.

"Did you see anybody go in my house?"

"No," I lie.

"They trashed my place and my spa room."

"What?" I act surprised.

"I called the police. I'm sick of this! I know it wasn't nobody but Pierre!"

"You tried calling him?"

"For what? All he gon' do is lie."

"Why would he do that, and he with your sister now?"

Her face hardens at my words. I know what I said stung like razor blades and hot sauce.

She doesn't bother entertaining what I said. Instead, she pulls out her phone.

"Hey, girl. I know you just left, but can you   come get me? Can I stay at your place for a bit? Someone just trashed my place."

I can't hear what's being said on the other end, but Pria lights up like a broke chick that scores forty dollars.

"I'm about to pack up what I can and get up out of here for a bit. I can't get ahead here."

"You gon' let them run you out of your place?"

"I place nothing above my peace of mind. Everything else can be replaced. Call me if you need me, Lotti."

"I won't."

She shrugs her shoulders and walks off. My friend is outgrowing me, and I hate the way that feels.

Even though I put up a good front like I'm good, the truth of the matter is that I'm not.

I battle depression daily. My life changed in an instant, now I'm left to figure it out. My dreams of being a mother, wife, and track coach have been snatched from me.

Mo is the only one who cares enough to pull me out of the funk. I push her so far away I doubt if she'll ever come back around.

Everyone gathers outside to see why the police are in the area without shots being fired.

They don't bother dusting for fingerprints or any of that. It's the hood, so stuff like this happen all the time. They always figure it's someone you know anyway.

They take her statement while her new friend holds her hand.

I refuse to be outshined, so I roll over to where they were.

"You good, Pria?"

"I will be. God keep making sure I don't get comfortable so I can keep pushing. Everything works out for the good of them that love the Lord."

Now she up here quoting scripture. I can't.

"Hi, I'm Meme." She extends her hand like we're at a job interview.

"Hey," my reply is as dry as a woman going through menopause.

Her right eyebrow raises, but she returns her attention back to Pria.

It's clear I'm not needed, so I went back to my house.

I watch out the window while Pria loads what she can in Meme's car and drove off.

I look down at my phone and read Pria's text message.

> *"Can you keep an eye on my apartment? I'll be back tomorrow to move the rest of my stuff into storage. I know you said you won't need me, but if you do, I'm always here, bestie."*

"Girl, bye," I scoff, throwing my phone.

I hear a light tapping on my door.

"Who is it?"

"P," he murmurs.

I snatch my door open. "Nigga, what you are doing here?"

"Girl, stop playing and give me a kiss."

"I ain't givin' you nothin'! I saw you and Nay goin' up in Pria's apartment earlier. Why y'all trashed her place?"

"That was still my place too. I didn't do nothing. That was her jealous sister."

"Well, you didn't stop her. Why you all up in my crib and you was just with her?"

"Because you been actin' stingy. Before your accident we used to get it in all the time. I told you I don't care about you being in a wheelchair. That just means you can't run anymore when I'm breaking your back," he laughs.

"Boy, shut up. I don't feel sexy like I used to then. This has all been an adjustment. Maybe God is punishing me for messing with you behind Pria back the last two years."

"Girl, that's nonsense. God ain't worried about us. C'mon, let me run you a bath and make you feel better."

Pria isn't with him anymore, so I can care less about him going behind Nay's back to be with me. I'm glad that me being paralyzed doesn't bother him. It's eating away at me and it'll feel good to be desired after all these months of adjusting.

P disappears into the bathroom and I can hear him start the bath.

"Girl, I'm about to spoil you tonight!" He shouts.

The corner of my mouth turns up.

"You need me to-"

"Nope, stay right in here," he stands in front of my wheelchair blocking my entrance to the back. "I got a surprise for you."

In about seven more minutes, he comes back.

"Your spa awaits you, my love," he has a towel draped over his arm like a butler.

Capria complains about Pierre so much but he's different with me. He isn't hard and thugged out. He shares his hopes and dreams with me.

I know exactly who he is, and I've never tried to change him. I just roll with whatever because he's never disrespected me. We are more like friends with benefits than anything. That's what works for us.

He picks me up and carries me into the bathroom. He lights my candles and the bubbles are running over the sides because he used so much.

"Let me get you undressed," he says.

"P, no!"

I panic when he offers to undress me. I'm still able to go to the bathroom on my own, but sometimes, I have to wear diapers just in case I can't make it in time.

"None of that bothers me, Lotti. Let me help you. I would never judge you or embarrass you."

"I'm just not ready for that quite yet. Can I have a minute to get myself straight, and I'll call you back in to wash me up. I want to hear how things are going now that you live with Nay." I laugh.

"That broad crazy."

"Yeah, just how you like them." I chuckle.

"Yeah, aight." He smacks his lips before closing the door.

I hold on the rail next to my toilet so I can lift my body up a little to pull my pants down. It takes some work, but I finally got undressed.

I sit on the edge of the tub and grab the other rail so I can lower my body in the bathtub. I slide down until I'm fully in.

"I'm in the tub, P."

"I was going to put you in the tub."

"I'm handicapped, but that doesn't mean that I'm not handicapable. I've been doing this for a lil' bit and it's made me even tougher. I can't be waiting around for people to come and rescue me."

"You right about that. But I'll always be here for you, Lotti."

"I see the way you treat women, so excuse me for not holding my breath waiting on you."

"Yeah, but I don't do you like that."

"You were with Capria for seven years, and she even did a bid with you. You still dogged that girl out."

"Cause she let me. I knew no matter what she would always take me back. I had love for Pria, but I'm not in love with her anymore. I fell out of love with her a long time ago. I love the hood like you, Lotti; Pria don't. Ain't no way that was gon' work. Yeah, I should've broke it off, but I know at the end of the day she solid and she'll do whatever for a nigga. It ain't right, but that's what it is."

"But I'm supposed to believe I'm different."

"You are different." He kisses my lips.

"I see your body still responds to me." His eyes fall to my hardened nipples.

"Shut-up." I splashed the water in his face.

"Lotisha, I will always love you, girl. I don't care if you believe me or not."

I know Pierre's lying, but I need to hear what he's saying. It's been a long time since someone has told me they love me.

My brother comes by once or twice a week to check on me, brings me groceries, and gives me money. He doesn't stay for long because the streets are always calling him for one reason or another.

After I got out of the tub, Pierre makes slow, sweet love to me. It isn't rushed but everything that I need.

Once we're done, he wraps me in his arms until I drift off to sleep. I know once I wake up, he'll be gone, but that's okay.

This will always be our little secret.

CHAPTER SIX

CAPRIA

Meme's house is located out by two forty-nine. It's still on the Northside but more suburban than being in the heart of Acres Home.

Her apartment is decorated but with a minimalist touch. I'm guessing because her brother was her roommate. She says he's going to be gone for several weeks training for the police academy.

There is a yellow couch and two turquoise chairs that are separated by a glass table. A white vase is in the center to accent the décor.

I'm glad it'll just be us two in the apartment. By the time he comes home, I should have my own little spot.

"Here, this is your room. Ezrah won't be here, so you can stay in his room."

"Okay, I should be out before he gets back."

"If not, then we'll figure it out. I'm sure he's going to be working crazy hours anyway. I don't care if you have to sleep with me like we some high school kids," she laughs. "Go ahead and get settled in."

I nod and sit on the bed. I have mixed feelings being in a new environment. I'm excited and scared all at one time. I wonder if Pierre is missing me yet?

I pull out my phone to text him. He hasn't been responding to me at all.

"Stop calling and texting him. You know he's the one that broke in your apartment. I know we haven't known each other an extremely long time, but baby, that's not it. The way that man treats you is toxic. He does it because you allow it. Why didn't you just put charges on him?"

"I didn't have proof, but I also don't want to put him back into the system. I can't do that. It will break him."

"He doesn't care about breaking you. So why should you care about breaking him?"

"I don't know, but I do."

"I would never judge you or make you feel bad about loving someone. I wouldn't be a friend if I didn't tell you that you deserved better either. A person who upholds you in when you're wrong doesn't care about you. Don't ever forget that."

"You don't understand. Won't nobody ever know Pierre the way I do. I know everything he's going to do before he does it."

"So, you knew he was going to break in your apartment and trash it?"

"No, but I knew he was going to lash out when I didn't blow him up once he left with my sister. He wanted my attention so he thought that would be one way to get it."

"Capria, that's not healthy. I'm begging you to love yourself enough to at least try to walk away."

"I'm going to try. It's going to help not living around a bunch of people who don't want nothing but the hood. I'm cut different, and they made me feel like something was wrong with me for wanting more."

"Ain't nothin' wrong with you, baby. You just have different desires. Desires that are going to change your life and the way you live. Just keep believing in yourself. I got your back all the way. I want to see you win, friend. I have something that will take your mind off Pierre. Are you familiar with the Black Lives Matter Movement?"

"Yeah, I've seen the protest and different people on social media speaking on their behalf."

"I'm a part of the local organization here. I want you to join with me."

"I don't know, Meme. That's not really my thing. Marching down these Houston streets in the heat demanding change that ain't gon' ever come."

"It's that thinking that's keeping our people stagnant. We have to stop thinking our vote and voice don't matter. I don't care how much they try and strip us of it, we're just going to get louder. We're just going to go harder. We have the power to make change happen if we come together."

Meme has gone into full Black Panther mode. I'm just sitting here in shock because she's always so mild mannered.

I've never witnessed this aggressive side of her. She's clearly passionate about Black Lives Matter.

"I'll go to a meeting with you. I'm not saying I will join or anything."

"Well, just had a meeting because we will be protesting tomorrow. That cop in Dallas is getting ready to get sentenced. We need to let the judicial system know that we want justice at all costs. We will not go silently into the night."

"Oookkaay," I slowly spit out.

"I'm sorry. I just love my people, and I'm done with these people making us feel like second class citizens in a country they built on our backs. No justice. No peace," she throws her fist in the air.

"So, should I wear all black and fluff out my afro orrrr?" I tease.

"Haha." She sticks her tongue out as she leaves the room.

I'm blocking Pierre on all social media and my phone while I have the guts. I know as soon as I see him calling, I'll just unblock him.

"No, you won't," I scold myself.

I just put my suitcase in the corner for the time being. Her brother has all of his stuff meticulously organized so I feel uncomfortable about touching any of his stuff.

I go over to his dresser and pick up his cologne. I put the Sauvage by Dior up to my nose and inhale. It smells heavenly. It instantly makes me want to get naked and bust it open.

The only time Pierre put on cologne is when he's going out.

*   *   *

There are so many people in attendance at the protest. Various poster boards are plastered with saying such as, "No justice. No peace. No racist police."

I'm paranoid. It looks like the perfect set-up for a shootout. Meme got me a shirt to wear. I walk alongside her while she yells, "All lives don't matter until black lives matter."

It's truly a sight to behold. The cops are here but didn't bother us as long as we we're peaceful. Some participants are yelling profanity at the cops, but they aren't reacting.

I don't know if it's because they understand or because of the news cameras filming.

They don't have to worry about Fox News reporting anything negative because they hate the Black Lives Matter movement. I'm not strong in it and can pick up on that much just from what they air.

Their newscasters are always so full of shade. I'm just taking it all in. I have no idea what I have gotten myself into. I'm inspired and the message is clear across the board. Change is needed!

We're all crowded in front of City Hall. News reporters are interviewing various people on why they're protesting.

It irritates me that some of them bypass those who can clearly articulate our reasoning for protesting and went straight to someone who is out there just to be there.

"We don't care if we have to burn this city to the ground. We will get justice."

"So you would burn down the city in which you live in the name of so-called justice?"

"If that's what it takes," the stranger ignorantly replies.

Meme sighs before marching over to the reporter.

"That is not what we are down here for. We are here to effect change in a non-violent manner. We are standing against those police officers who believe they are above the law. We stand against those who sully the perception of those who do put on that uniform every day and protect their communities. We are not against police officers. We are against police brutality." She shoves the mic back into the reporter's hand before storming off.

"Well, I guess you told her." I snicker.

"Girl, they get on my nerves trying to portray all of us as violent vigilantes."

"Well, you didn't let that ride."

"You can't. We have to protect the way they portray us in the media at all costs. They are trying to label us as a terrorist group."

"What?"

"Terrorism is defined as the use of violence and intimidation in pursuit of political aims. That's not what we're about. Everyone that screams Black Lives Matter is not necessarily a part of our organization."

"If that's the case then why hasn't the KKK been deemed a terrorist organization? Asking for fair treatment doesn't automatically deem us as terrorists!"

"Exactly. This is an uphill battle, but we're not letting up. I won't push you to join, but I hope you can understand the difference you can make."

"I promise to think more about it. Can you take me to find something to wear for graduation next week after we go and put my stuff in storage?"

"I sure can. Let's go to your place now and get that taken care of before it gets dark. Let me make a quick stop by my daddy house and grab his truck."

"He's going to let you use his truck?"

"My daddy never tells me no, girl." She fiddles with her earring.

We pulled up and her dad was sitting outside drinking on a cold Budweiser.

"Hey daddy baby," he called out to Meme before she could get up the driveway good.

"Hey daddy," she kissed him on the cheek and hugged him tightly. "Daddy, I need to use your truck to help my friend move."

"Is that so? Your friend doesn't speak?"

"Hell…hello," I stuttered.

"Hey there. You can come closer. I don't bite."

I smiled but didn't move from leaning on Meme's car.

"She a lil' scary something ain't she?"

"Daddy, leave my friend alone."

"You know where the keys are. Bring it back in one piece."

I was relieved and also wonder what it felt like to have a father's love.

My father died in an insane asylum when me and my sister were teenagers. My mom says he isn't right after the war when he came home.

When I pull up to my apartment, I was glad that nothing else was trashed.

Pierre had sold almost anything of value, so I didn't have anything large to pack.

What I can salvage of my spa equipment, I load into the large tote I bought at Wal-Mart.

I don't have a lot of food or clothes, so it only takes us a couple of hours. Pierre took his stuff when he broke in so that's one less thing I have to deal with.

"So, you really movin' out?"

Lotti is at the bottom of the stairs when I came down with my last load of stuff.

Meme is a big help. When I brought the stuff down she would stack it neatly in her dad's truck.

"Yep. I'm really moving out."

"Why you act like you too good for the hood now? You're getting new friends, going to that stuck up school on the other side of town, and you don't go to any of the trail rides anymore."

"I don't go to the trail rides because my best friend got shot at one."

"Best friend, huh? It looks like you have a new best friend to me."

"I can have more than one best friend."

"No, you can't."

"Says who?"

"I say."

"Lotti, I'm not trying to argue with you. As my friend you should want me to do better. It's toxic here for me. I can't heal with my ex and sister flaunting themselves in my face."

"I hear you. Just don't forget where you come from and who really love and loyal to you. That's all I'm saying."

"I won't. Here, this is for you."

"What's this?"

"An invitation to my graduation next week."

"I don't think I'll be able to make it."

"You didn't even check to see what day it is." I pinch the bridge of my nose. "You know what? You don't have to come. Take care, Lotti." I snatch my invitation from her and get in the truck with Meme.

"Are you okay?"

"Yeah, I just hate what that wheelchair has done to her."

"Something tells me this didn't start when she got in that chair. I'm sure she's been shady but you've overlooked it for so long you're numb to it. She probably became blunter once she got in that chair." I'm being quiet because she's right. I always make excuses for Lotti. It started way before her accident too.

I need to stop letting people treat me like trash. I feel like folks around me use my loyalty against me. Meme is the only person I've been around that genuinely wants to see me win.

My mama is not against me doing better but she makes me feel like it's my responsibility to help my sister.

I did my part of helping raise her while she worked all the time. My sister is a grown woman. We lived in the same house. We ate the same food. We were exposed to the same environment. She chose the path that she's on and she can change it when she really wants to.

For now, I'm staying away from all of them. My mama said she was coming to my graduation, so I'm excited about that. She always tells me she's proud of me.

Next week my life will change for the better. I already have a job lined up at a spa near Meme's apartment. I really like the area. It's a lot of traffic that travels on two forty-nine. I should be able to build up my clientele. Once I save enough money for my own spot, I can take them with me.

I already have a bit of branding I'll be doing on the sly. Like my personal slogan, signature massage technique, and I'll be perfecting my skin care line.

I have a plan, and I'm going to stick to it no matter what.

CHAPTER FIVE

EZRAH

18 Weeks Later

The police academy dug off in my butt. I'm relieved to be home, but I have to be at work the following day to meet with my field training officer. Iza says she's trained to be one but doesn't know if they will assign me to her yet.

I got in town early so I didn't bother to call Meme. I wanted to surprise her anyway.

I'm doing my best to keep quiet so I won't wake her. I'm not in the mood to hear her mouth.

I stick my head in Meme's room, and she's sound asleep. I did the same thing when I got in at night. I would make sure she was safe in her bed.

One thing I'm grateful for is that my baby sister isn't a club rat. She's about school, her money, and loving those connected to her unapologetically.

I shut the door back to her bedroom and go into mine.

"What the h-" some random chick standing in the middle of the floor half naked yells.

I can tell her jewel-like eyes are shooting daggers my way even in the dimly lit room. Her skin is the color of gingerbread and smooth. Her face is drawn in rage but the dimple in her chin remains. Her white teeth are clenched and gleaming. The cut above her lip is noticeable but not ugly. I wonder what happened?

"Who are you?"

"Who are *you*?"

"Um, you're in my room," I inform her.

Her eyes widen. "Well, can you please turn around so I can put my shirt on?"

"Sure. My bad. I'm Ezrah, by the way."

"I'm Capria. I'm Meme's friend from school. She's been letting me crash here while I get on my feet."

"She thought we had a few more days before you got back from the academy."

"Ezrah? Hey, big bro." She leaps into my arms. "I see you two have already met."

"Not funny. Girl, I was in here half naked." She draws a sharp breath.

"You ain't got nothin' that Ezrah hasn't seen. I told you he was a first responder." She giggles.

She twirls in a circle. "I don't care! He ain't seen nothin' packaged as nicely as this!"

Meme's little friend is something else.

"Well, I can take the couch." I tell them.

"No, I can't let you do that. I was about to go for my morning jog anyway. By the time I get back it'll be time for me to get to work. I have enough money to get my own place, so I shouldn't be here much longer."

"Don't be silly. I can clear out my office and we can turn that into your room. I know you're trying to get your own spot for your business. I say make that happen then focus on getting your own spot," Meme tells her.

My sister is always trying to help people. I hope this so-called friend isn't using her.

"I hope you're not just using my sister." I shoot her a venomous look.

"Using her? Who do you think you are coming in here attacking me for no reason? You don't even know me!"

"Ezrah, she's not like that! Stop treating me like I don't have a mind of my own. I'm not this gullible little girl you perceive me to be."

"I would never use or do anything to hurt Meme. She's the only friend that I have that hasn't betrayed or belittled me. Not that it's any of your business. I'm going on my run." She skewers me with an unflinching look.

She darts out of the door without looking back.

"Why did you treat her that way, Ezrah?"

"You know why."

"Look, you brought Alysia around me. How was I supposed to know she was just using me to get to you? I didn't know someone would go to such lengths just to get the attention of a man. Capria doesn't even know your dusty self, boy!"

"Duuustttyyy?"

"You heard me. You need to apologize to her when she gets back. Help me move my computer desk and computer to my room before you lay down."

"We have to do all of that now? Meme, I just got in town."

"I want to get at least that done before Pria gets back. When she gets off I want us to go shopping for her a bedroom set or at least a bed."

"You really like her, huh?"

"Yes, I do. She's worked hard to build her self-esteem back up after the people she used to have around her tried to destroy her. They envied and punished her for wanting better. I've been showing her there's a better way to live. That she's worthy of love, Ezrah."

"She's not a project or a pet, Meme."

"I didn't say she was. I love her like a sister I never had, Ezrah. Just trust me on this."

"I will. For now."

By the time Capria makes it back from her run, I've finished moving the stuff out of the office.

"She didn't have to do this," she sighs, leaning against the doorway of the office.

"When Meme loves someone, she loves them hard. I'm sorry for the way I spoke to you. My sister had been through some rough friendships in the past."

"Well, I'm not like them. Don't bother apologizing. You've already revealed that you like to judge people you don't know. You assumed I was like others your sister has encountered in the past. You've succeeded at leaving a bad taste in my mouth, Ezrah. You might as well save your breath."

CHAPTER SEVEN

EZRAH

I come to the entrance designated for officers as instructed. The electric doors click open allowing me access.

"Where do I find the chief's office?"
"Go straight down the hall. You will pass the dispatchers and his office is in the far right corner."

"Thank you."

I follow the instructions I'm given. I could hear the murmur of the dispatchers as I pass them. The area near the chief's office smells like old coffee.

I knock on the door.

"Come in!" he yells from the other side.

"Hello, sir. I'm Ezrah Marshall."

"Report to the debriefing room. I will be there shortly." He doesn't even bother lifting his head to make eye contact.

The portly Caucasian man is already giving me bad vibes. I hope I'm wrong.

There are about four other new officers sitting in the room. One is leaning back in his rolling chair so far; I think he's going to fall over.

I take a seat in the back so I can see everyone in the room. The white dry erase board read, "Welcome New Recruits".

I'm the only black cop in the room, and I've noticed so far only a handful on the force. It isn't a career on the top ten list of a minority.

"Welcome to the force." The chief walks in. Even though I'm in the far back corner, I can smell the smoke wafting off his uniform. "You will be in the classroom today, and tomorrow you will be paired with your field officer. I must warn you that tensions are high with the recent death of Botham Jean. The city is in an uproar, and we need to be on guard. Looting has started in the downtown area, so most of the force is there."

"When will those people learn that violence is not the answer?" one of the rookies asks.

"Those people?" I respond.

"Don't come in here being overly sensitive. You know what I meant."

"Yeah, I know exactly what you meant! That's why people are protesting now!"

"You better understand now that you are blue, not black, boy," he snaps.

"Who are you calling, boy?" I stood from my seat."

"Hey, cool it, guys. We must always have each other's back. The enemy is in the streets, not on the force!"

The chief is basically reinforcing that we're blue bloods.

"Why don't you all take a break," the chief suggests. "Officer Marshall, can you hang back?"

"Yes, Chief?"

He waits until everyone is out of the room. "You don't want to make it hard on yourself on the force, son. I don't agree with his approach, but he's right. You are a blue blood now. Race doesn't matter here. It's more of them than us on the street. When I say them, I mean criminals."

"I hear you."

"I hope so. I've gone through your file and it's impeccable. As a first responder you have several letters of recommendations including one from the commander here. You can easily advance up the ranks if you know how to play ball."

"Thanks, Chief."

"Now go ahead and take a break so you can cool your head. Some of these officers are jerks, but any one of them will give their life for you if they know you're loyal to the force."

I nod in understanding and go outside to take my break.

After a gruelling eight-hour training session, I'm glad to be home. The apartment is quiet when I get there, but Meme's car is outside.

I take my things into my room and change clothes.

I poured myself some raspberry lemonade and take a seat on the patio to clear my mind.

"Are you okay?"

I turned around at the sound of Capria's voice.

"Yeah."

"Look, I know we got off to a rough start, but I can tell you had a back day. I've had that same look plenty of days. You want to talk about it?"

"It was my first day on the force officially today. Another rookie made a comment about the protesters, and I checked him. My chief pulled me to the side during break and told me basically I need to play ball if I want them to have my back. He said with my impeccable file as a first responder I can easily advance."

"Are you going to do it?"

"I don't think I have a choice. I need them to watch my back out there in the field. I don't want to end up on the other end of their guns or left to the slaughter."

"I hear you. With the murder of Botham Jean, I will tell you now that it has worked the world as we know it. Black people are looking at black cops like traitors. They feel like y'all are standing by letting them kill us because y'all bleed blue. Y'all want us to understand that y'all are black and deal with injustice on the force, but y'all won't take a stand. Most of y'all refuse to speak out. What's happening is modern day lynching's via guns. I bet a lot of your fellow officers are nothing but KKK members with badges."

"I don't know about all that, but I've only been on the force one day. I can't attest to all of that. To be honest, I don't know what I would do if I had to speak up against injustice. I feel like I would stand my ground no matter what, but I don't know what's it's like on the force yet. I don't know what backlash I would be facing doing it."

"I hear you."

"You know the rodeo in town. Would you like to go with me?"

"Why?"

"My sister is crazy about you so I think it would be wise to get to know you for myself," I laughed.

"Yes, I would like to go with you."

Her posture goes limp, as if all her bones have dissolved away, leaving only her skin to make do with sitting in the chair.

"What's wrong?" I asked her.

"I know this is not a date but I have never gone out with anyone but my ex."

"I'm out of practice as well, so I'm sure you will be fine. Just be yourself. I can tell when people aren't authentic or lying."

"I don't know if that was a warning, threat, or information, but I'll be ready."

"Sounds good."

"Well, I'll leave you to your thoughts. Don't let those people get to you, and I know if the time ever comes, you will do what's right." She smiles.

CHAPTER EIGHT

CAPRIA

The dirt arena surrounded by bleachers has my heart jumping like a trampoline. I'm like a kid when it comes to going to the rodeo. It's every Houstonian's rite of passage. They pay top dollar to have artists come and perform, and the food was bomb.

"So, what should we eat first?"

"You sound really greedy." She smiles from ear to ear.

"Well, I'm starting with a turkey leg."

"Me too! I want some boudin too! And shrimp on a stick!"

"Now who greedy?"

"Oh my God! A mechanical bull! I have to get on it!"

"Well, I was a first responder, so when you fall and bust your butt, I got your back."

"Prepare to be amazed, grasshopper."

I hand the attendant a five-dollar-bill and hop on the oversized air mat surrounding the bull.

I climb up the right side of the bull and pull myself up using my upper body strength.

I position myself and grip the horn of the saddle. I nod to the operator and mechanical bull gently rotates. First left, then right, and a final circle.

I roll my hips and let them give with the direction of the bull. As speed increases, I tighten my grip. The bull increases with such force, it leans on its axis. I slide to the side but never release me grip. A crowd starts to gather because they're amazed at how long I stay on.

The crowd starts to cheer me on. The hating operator hit a button which causes the bull to violently jerk to the right.

My four-foot-eleven petite frame flies off the bull.

"Bwwhahaha." I erupt in laughter.

"Are you okay?"

Ezrah is hovering over me. His breath smells like Spearmint.

"Yeah, I just got a bit of dust in my throat," I cough.

"Well, that won't kill you. You were amazing up there."

"Thank you. Don't go telling everybody my secret talent now. I don't need all the perves in my inbox."

"Your secret is safe with me. Promise."

"Let's get you something to eat."

We finally find turkey legs. We've just missed the cattle roping competition so the small bleachers are empty.

I'm an introvert, so I can only be around crowds in waves. I'm relieved to get a break.

"So, what are your ambitions? Do you want to be a police officer for the rest of your life?"

"I want to be a detective ultimately. I have a long road ahead of me but I know it will be worth it. I want to protect people from the monsters in the world."

"Being a detective allows you to do that?"

"Yes, and I can give victims and families closure. What about you?"

"I want to own my own spa. That's why your sister is adamant about me staying with y'all. She believes in me so strongly that I can't help but to believe in myself. I'm saving every penny to get a small shop. Once it flourishes, I plan to expand then eventually have a few on each side of Houston."

"That sounds dope. I need to come get me a facial or something."

"I'm already a licensed massage therapist too. I got my certification as an aesthetician to expand the services I offer my clients. I have a plan. I just need to stay focused. I'll be the first in my family to own a business."

"That's dope." He anchors his attention on me. "I need to get back home so I can go in to work tonight. I wish we could hang out longer. I've enjoyed your company."

"You don't think it's weird that I live with y'all? What if this goes left or something? It's going to be awkward seeing each other every day."

"We just came to the rodeo. I don't think we have to worry about that quite yet."

"You're right. I'm always over analysing things. I hate surprises so I'm always trying to look ahead at the what ifs."

"It's cool. I haven't dated in a while, and Meme told me you just gettin' out of a relationship too."

"Dang it, Meme." My head flies back.

"No, she didn't go into detail. She just said you just broke up with your guy."

"Oh."

"Meme's loyal. She wouldn't betray your trust even to me. That's just her. She's always wanted a sister, and I think she's found one in you."

"Oh, you don't think I'm just trying to use her anymore?"

"I'm sorry about that. For real. I've just watched her get her heart broken many times trying to help so called friends. I told you that I can tell when people are being authentic, and you are."

"Thanks."

The drive back home is chill. India Swan's song *Movin' On* fills the atmosphere in the car with good vibes.

"I really enjoyed myself today," I tell Ezrah before we get out the car.

"So did I."

When we get to the front door, we hear Meme arguing with someone.

Ezrah rushes by me and opens the door.

"Alysia, what are you doing here?"

"Violating is what she's doing! She lucky I got too much to lose or I would've put my hands on her!"

"Girl, you ain't stupid. I see you already movin' on. Well, you might as well get used to seeing me, sweety, because I'm about to be his baby mama." She rubs her stomach.

"We're just friends, so you can save the theatrics, honey." I give a half shrug and walk through them and take a seat on the couch.

I want to take in all this tea. Ezrah isn't my man, but I want to know everything this chick has to vomit out of her mouth.

"She's a cocky one, isn't she?"

"You have no idea." I smile.

"Leave her out of this," Ezrah speaks up. "What do you mean you're pregnant? We used protection every time despite you being on the shot."

"Well, anything is possible. I just wanted you to know. This is definitely your sister because she was just as adamant as you that this wasn't your child. She acts like she was there holding the flashlight when we were having sex. She up in here actin' like your trained guard dog."

"Look, leave my sister out of this! You said what you had to say. I need to go with you to the doctor for a pregnancy test and then a DNA test."

"DNA test? Seriously?"

"Seriously. We've been broken up for a few months now."

"And I'm three months pregnant."

"Sure you are," Meme interjects.

"Mind your business. You come out of your shell and you could get someone to spread those rusty legs of yours."

"I'll leave the slutting up to you, ma'."

"Yeah, whatever."

"Alysia, you need to leave. Now!"

"Fine, but I'll be in touch." She flashes a peace sign.

She's a weird one, I'll give her that.

I knew Ezrah was too good to be true. Men always have some drama lurking in the closet.

At least I've found out before this went any further. I'm trying to stay away from drama as much as possible.

I know Meme says I can stay here, but just as I suspect, things will get awkward. I'll spend tonight on Apartments.com finding me a nice efficiency apartment for now. I don't need anything fancy, just somewhere to lay my head for now.

"I'm sorry about all this." Ezrah's shoulders slump.

"It's cool. It was just the rodeo." I flash a fake smile.

I go into my room and lay on my bed. I look down at my phone and still nothing from Pierre. I was sure he would be begging get back with me by now.

My life is getting better, but I'll be lying if I say I didn't miss him.

I hoped that things went a little better with Ezrah. He's ambitious and passionate. I love the way he loves his sister.

Realistically, I have a full plate. There's no place for love right now. I need to get to this money. There's a life I'm destined to live, and it only comes through grinding.

CHAPTER NINE

EZRAH

I know I told Capria that the rodeo was basically just us hanging out, but I'm feeling her. She's feisty, but her drive, personality, and natural beauty have me intrigued. I'm not ready to jump in another relationship, but it would be nice to get to know her better.

I didn't see her for the rest of the night yesterday after everything that happened. Meme was in her room with her, but she didn't say anything about what they talked about.

She's right about one thing; it has become weird. I need to get my own place. I'm too old to be sharing a spot with my sister anyway.

I feel better knowing that Capria will be here with her. They can keep each other safe.

I call the spa Capria works at and schedule a massage with her. What better way to break the tension than her seeing all this sexy chocolate naked under a towel?

I have to change her association with me. I don't keep up drama or have women popping out of the shadows.

If she chooses not to get to know me better, it will be for the right reasons, not the wrong ones.

When I walk into the spa, the smell of sandalwood hit me in the face. There's a pitcher sitting on the glass table filled with ice, lemon, and cucumbers. The sound of running water is being played through the speakers in the lobby.

"My name is Ezrah Marshall, I have an appointment with Capria."

"Yes, she'll be right out to get you."

Before I can sit down, Capria is already coming out to get me."

"Mr. Marshall, you can come this way."

"I'm sorry for popping up at your job."

"No, you're not. What I want to know is why are you here? This is weird. We went to the rodeo and that was it. There's no reason for you to be coming up to my place of employment."

"I just wanted to explain more about yesterday."

"That's your business, not mine. Please get undressed, and you better not stiff me on my tip since you decided to fill one of my spots today. I'm always booked, so I'm surprised you were even able to get an appointment."

"It must be fate."

"No, the devil is persistent too."

"I see."

"I'll step out so you can get undressed. You can cover your lower half with this towel."

She handed me a plush white towel. I don't know what type of fabric softener they use, but it makes the towel feel like cotton.

I follow her instructions and sit on the massage table. It's firm but didn't seem like it will be uncomfortable.

"You can lay down on the table. Would you like to listen to running water, bird sounds, rain, or dolphins?"

"Rain. I love the rain."

She doesn't respond. Her soft hands kneading my flesh feels astounding. I can feel the knots of tension rolling between her fingertips.

"I know you had ulterior motives coming here, but your body needed this. You have so many knots in your back."

"I carry my stress in my shoulders. I want you to know I'm moving out this week. Don't tell Meme. I want to be the one to tell her."

She stops massaging me. "You don't have to leave your home. I've already started looking for a place."

"I'm too old to be living with my sister. I feel better now that you're there with her. Y'all can work on building y'all lil' empires," I chuckle. "Y'all probably can host a few of those Black Lives Matter meetings at the crib now that a cop won't be coming through."

"Shut up." She slaps my back.

"Ouch. That stung, girl."

"Be still so I can finish."

The air whooshing through the vent enhances the peacefulness of the spa. I see now why people always came here. She might as well get ready to see me every other week. This is addictive.

I stare at the fresh cut flowers in the vase as my thoughts carry me away. I'm not thinking about anything in particular. Just hoping that my career and love life will flourish and shine just like those flowers.

CHAPTER TEN

CAPRIA

Five Months Later

It's been almost six months since me and Pierre have been broken up. I still haven't heard from Lotti. I text her and have tried calling a few times after I moved in with Meme, but she never responds or picks up. I'm not going to beg anyone to be friends with me. Lotti is immature, and I've been doing the work to purge myself of all my toxic traits. Despite Ezrah coming to the spa for his bi-weekly massages, we've been keeping it platonic.

I'm still stacking my money for my spa and Meme is loving her new job as a Crime Scene Cleaner for the most part. But some days she comes home so broken and cries all night.

Some of those scenes are so gruesome and the stories behind them are even more heartbreaking. Her most recent clean was of a husband who shot his wife in front of their two children. It was told to the police that she wanted a divorce and he couldn't handle it.

She felt they had outgrown each other and wanted them to go their separate ways.

"Capira, do you think you can close tonight? I'm sorry about the last minute request, but my daughter locked herself out of the house."

"Megan, you know that's no problem at all."

"Thank you so much. You remember the code, right?"

"Yes, I do. Stop acting like a Nervous Nelly. I've closed so many times I can't believe you still act like this." I give a dismissive wave of my hand and go back to cleaning. "Hold up. Did Lizzie book another late appointment today?"

"Um..yeah." Megan wrinkles her nose.

"That's why you're acting like this. Why do you keep letting her do that? How late?"

"She should be done at eight."

I tilt my head back so that I'm looking at the ceiling. "Why, Lord? Why?"

"You'll be aight," Megan laughs before disappearing out the room.

I can hear the doors click as Megan locks them on her way out.

I look at the clock, and I only have about forty-five more minutes to go.

By the time I'm finished cleaning my room, she should be done.

I sanitize my bed, walls, equipment, and chairs. Covid-19 changes how we do business. We really just opened back up to clients, but they have to have masks on.

We all agreed to Covid tests before we came back. I still wear my mask at all times. I don't care if I can't breathe.

So far it's all working out. Business picks back up, but I'm grateful to have some money saved up. Meme is considered an essential employee, so she never stops working. I worry about her so much when the outbreak first happened. Her job was dangerous enough without a viral outbreak.

"I'm ready, girl." Lizzie sticks her head in the door.

"Okay, let me grab my purse."

I go in my closet and grab my things.

I put my mask on and turn out the lights in my massage room.

"I turned off the lights already," Lizzie says.

That's the least she could do. Got me here all night waiting on her.

"Lizzo, you really need to stop booking your last appointment so late. It's not fair for us to have to keep waiting for you. Anything could hap-"

"Get back inside!"

We are coming out of the store, and I don't have enough time to say or do anything. There's someone in front of us. Someone with a mask covering their face. The masked stranger has a gun pointed at us. I'm so scared all I can see is that gun. He has some kind of voice altering device against his throat.

"Please, we don't keep any money here," Lizzie lies.

"She's right," I lie with her.

"It better be something in here so y'all don't die for nothing."

There is something familiar about the man robbing us. I can tell he's disguising his voice but something is off. I'm too scared to figure it out though.

"Where is the safe?" he yells.

"It's behind the counter," Lizzie cries.

"One of you open it! I know somebody got the code because y'all closin'! I will kill both of you dead, so don't try me!"

Lizzie and I look at each other. Tears are pouring out our eyes. His words grow legs, kick me in the chest, driving all the breathable air from my body.

I slowly lean down and enter the combination.

"The only cash accessible is what we use throughout the week if a customer needs change. We make drops throughout the day, and this inside safe won't open until the morning." I point it out to him.

"How much is that?"

"What? The cash right there?"

"Yeah! Are you slow or something?"

"It's two thousand dollars."

"Move out my way." He keeps the gun pointed at us and fills a plastic bag he takes out his picket with the other. "Lay on the ground face down and count to fifty," he demands.

We do as he asks and pray he isn't going to shoot us execution style.

When we hear the door alarm notify us we know he's gone.

"Oh my God," Lizzie panics.

I run to the door and lock it. I scramble over to my bag to get my cell phone.

"We've just been robbed," I blurt through the phone to the dispatcher.

I give her as many details as I can but I'm not much help.

Within fifteen minutes, the cops are speeding into the parking lot.

"Are you okay?" Ezrah rushes through the door.

"Yeah, I'm okay."

"I won't rest until I find out who did this!"

"Calm down, super cop. Let's find out how much they know first," the lady I assume is his partner says.

"Pria, this is Ivy, my partner. What can you tell us about what just happened?"

"He used some type of device to disguise his voice. It was strange."

"No, it was probably someone one of you knew."

"I doubt it," Lizzie scoffs.

"I haven't been anywhere for the last five months but work. I literally don't go anywhere unless I'm with Meme," I tell them.

"Most burglars don't use voice modifiers," Ivy says.

"He wore a mask and he had on a black hat. He was about five-nine with a medium build."

"Did you notice any distinguishing marks or tattoos?"

"No," we answer in unison.

"Do either of you need medical attention?" Ezrah asks.

"They look fine to me." I don't miss the indifferent glance she tosses s around the room at us.

I don't know what her problem is but this is why our people don't trust cops that look like us.

"Can I talk to you for a moment?" Ezrah asks.

"Sure."

He pulls me over to a corner to the other end of the room.

"Pria, I think Pierre did this."

"You don't even know him like that to toss around that accusation. I haven't seen or talked to him for months."

"That doesn't mean he hasn't been keeping tabs on you, Capria. That man was hell bent on destroying you, and it didn't work. Maybe he circled back to finish the job."

"I can't believe you."

"Tell me where I can find him then so I can ask him some questions."

"I won't do that. The last thing I'm going to do is put a black man in the crosshairs of the cops. A simple questioning will turn into him getting shot dead in the street like an animal. Thanks, but no thanks. You're going to have to earn your pay today. Do some investigative work since you want to be a detective one day. This will be great practice."

His face remains a plank of wood, his amazement hidden by a slow breath.

"Come on, Ivy. We're done here," he says, storming out the door.

The forensic team is done already taking pictures and fingerprints.

"We'll wait outside until you lock up."

Lizzie is outside on the phone with Megan I assumed.

I lock up and set the alarm.

"What did Megan say?"

"She was freaking out and trying to come down here. I told her we took care of it, and we would bring her up to speed tomorrow. She was worried about us."

"Well, I hope she stops letting you make these late appointments! You almost got us killed tonight!"

I hope my words blow her thin edges off! I tell Megan time and time again it's a bad idea letting her have late appointments!

*   *   *

I squeeze my eyes closed because I'm determined to sleep in today. Megan gave us the day off after what happened. She told us to just come by before the spa closed today.

I finally grab my phone and it's an unknown number. I answer because it can be a potential client. I've been passing my business card to my faithful clients to pass to their people.

"This is Capria," I was trying not to sound as if I've been up all morning.

"Turn your white voice off. It's me, Nay."

"Nay, what do you want?"

I haven't talked to my sister since she took my man. The only reason I'm staying on the phone is to make sure our mom and my nephews are okay.

"I just thought you should know that Pierre is sleeping with Lotti."

"Girl, get off my phone with that mess."

"No, I'm serious, Pria. You know how much they talk around there. So I went and kicked her door in. Sure enough he was laying in the bed with that half-dead body trick."

"Bye, Nay. It's called Karma, and she doesn't discriminate. It's just your turn now so just roll with it like I did." I hang up the phone in her face.

I text Ezrah Lotti's address letting him know he might be able to find P there. I also send him Nay's address just in case she decides to let him come back.

He responds with a simple thank you to let me know he's received it.

I hop out the bed and throw on some joggers and a t-shirt.

I finally have my own car and I'mglad for times like these. I can just pop up when I want to.

"Meme, I'll be right back."

"Okay," she mumbles and turn back over pulling the covers over her head.

I shoot over to Greenspoint in a matter of minutes.

BAM!

BAM!

BAM!

I'm beating on Lotti's door like the police. She finally opens the door.

"Oh, your jealous sister called you. She gotta be in her feelings to call you."

"So, it's true? You sleepin' with P now too?"

"Now? Girl, we've been screwing since he got out on this last bid. He was with you the day he got out and with me the next while you were at work. This ain't just start. You just findin' out about it."

"How is he screwing you? Your legs don't even work. Before, yeah, I can see it. Now?"

"Well, this coochie work, and he be swimmin' in it." She turns to me, her face lighting up as she speaks.

"You were supposed to be my friend. You held me while I cried when he cheated on me and dogged me out."

"I know, and it was exhausting. Your stupid self-kept taking him back."

"He's going to do the same thing to you."

"The difference between the two of us is that I know who he is. I ain't tryna change P. That's why I don't have to beg him to do anything or come around. He's free with me."

"We'll see how long that lasts."

"What is that supposed to mean?"

"I'll let you be surprised like I was. You two deserve each other."

Pffhh.

I know this tramp ain't just spit on me!

"You stupid trick!"

I snatch Lotti by her hair and drag her out of her wheelchair and pounce on her.

She reaches up and tries to grab my throat, but I catch her in her mouth.

"Get off me!" She screams.

"Nah, you want to spit on somebody, now you can enjoy these hands."

I'm wearing her out. My arms ache from the fighting. My hand cramps, but I hold myself strong.

I didn't dog her the way she deserves, but I show her mercy because she's handicapped.

"The next time you decide to spit on somebody make sure you got somebody to help you," I spit back on her and went and got in my car.

I'm waiting on Lil' Marco to call me so I can give him a piece of my mind, too.

I know once he finds out what she did, he won't do anything.

"What happened?" Meme asks once I storm through the door.

I'm a mess. I'm covered in blood and tears are running down my cheeks.

"Lotti," I pant.

"Is she okay?"

"She's messing with Pierre now," I cry.

"Oh, honey." She pulls me into her arms.

"I can't believe this!"

"You know Ezrah is feeling you. Why are you so afraid to move on from Pierre? This man keeps ripping your heart out and stepping on it."

"Meme, I'm not about to deal with a baby mama for the next eighteen years."

"He will never be with her even if she's pregnant. I believe she's lying, but that's neither here nor there. He's going to ask you out again. Say yes."

"I don't think I'm ready for all that, Meme."

"I'm not asking you to force it, but at least try to move on with your life, Pria."

"I'll try. I promise."

"Have you seen the video?"

"What video?"

Her handshakes as she reaches for her phone. She goes to a page on social media and presses play. Tears, rage, and heartbreak washes over me like a plague.

I watch a cop kill a man in the street like his life doesn't matter. My tears reveal the pain in my soul as he cries for his mother.

"Where is his mom?" I ask Meme.

"She's dead. She's been dead for a while."

"Oh my God! This is too much. When does it stop, Meme? They're slaughtering us, and no one is doing anything about it!"

"We're going to do something. We're going to protest. Not like we've been doing, but it's up there now, Pria. We're going to make them feel our pain. We are going to stop giving them our business and support black businesses only, we're going to take over the streets, we're going occupy City Hall, and we're voting!"

I just shake my head. I'm in a trance. This can't be life in the twenty-first century. I remember my granny telling us about her civil rights days. Here we are still fighting. Heading to get in good trouble.

CHAPTER ELEVEN

EZRAH

Pria sounded a bit down when I invited her to the aquarium today. I was shocked that she even accepted. I've been working a lot but when she sent me the information about Pierre, it showed me she was trying to move forward. She explained to me they had been together for quite some time. I understand more than anyone the difficulty she's having.

She said she would meet me here but she was already an hour late.

I try calling her but her phone goes straight to voicemail.

"Seriously?"

People slow down to make sure they hear me talking to myself.

"Mind your business," I snap at them.

I should've known that she would stand me up. She didn't seem like herself when I spoke to her on the phone.

It works out for the best because they're calling all hands on deck. The death of George Floyd has ignited this world. Millions of people watched a man be murdered in the street in front of witnesses.

My uniform feels heavier putting it on today. My gun feels colder and my stomach is in knots.

I have no idea of what I will encounter in the streets today as a cop or a black man.

Racism has always been the dead body hidden in the basement of the United States.

The smell got so funky someone finally dug it up and exposed it for what it is.

The white people are even enraged and voicing the displeasure with law enforcement.

A group of police officers sprinkled across America have consistently doused gasoline on this fire. Now the world has combusted in flames.

This fire won't be easily extinguished. Not this time.

I stop by Meme's house on my way to work to make sure she isn't planning on going to the protest downtown.

"Meme!" I yell, walking in their apartment.

"Why are you doing all that yelling?" She runs from the back room.

"I was checking to see if you were here."

"Where else I'm going to be?"

Pria slowly creeps out of her room. They're wearing matching Black Lives Matter shirts.

"Y'all can't go down to that protest tonight! It's not going to be safe. Not all of those protesters are going to be peaceful."

"Maybe that's what this city needs!" Meme snaps.

"We don't need to tear up our own city to prove a point! We have to live here! There are just as many black businesses downtown. You think they're going to pass them up or protect them? Don't go down there, Meme! You either, Pria!"

"Listen, you can tell your sister what to do, not me."

"I care about your safety, too. You know how I feel about you, so don't do that. The last thing I need is for either of you to get caught in the crossfire."

"You bleed blue, Ezrah. I can't speak for Meme, but your loyalty is divided. You ain't all in with the movement. You're really an op to be honest."

"Listen, don't come spewing that propaganda at me. Being an officer is my job not my ethnicity. You would be smart not to confuse the two or ever come at me like that again."

I leave them standing there looking stupid. If they want to go into that war zone, that's on them.

CHAPTER TWELVE

CAPRIA

Ezrah came up in here tripping for no reason. We're not going to stop what we've been doing just because it's up there with the death of George Floyd. If anything we're about to go harder!

"Are we still going downtown Meme?"

"Yeah, ain't nothin' changed. Ezrah know what these cops on, so of course he doesn't want us downtown, but we have a duty to our people! We can't keep talking about change and not act. Let's go so we can get a parking spot."

We listen on the radio as they recap what's going on downtown. So far, it sounds as if everything is going peacefully.

We find a parking spot and jump out.

"Here, take this." Meme hands me a taser.

"What do I need this for?"

"Listen, not everyone is here for the right reasons. Some people just want to use this as an excuse to act a fool. Somebody comes at you sideways then you tase them fools in the stomach or mouth."

"The mouth?" I laugh.

"Hey, whatever will get them up off of you."

I stuff the taser in my back pocket and grab my poster board.

There are so many of us gathering together. It's so dope.

"Who are they?"

"Girl, I don't know…" Meme's words trail off.

The only way to describe the army of black soldiers dressed like new age Black Panthers is show stopping. Each of them are armed, disciplined, and confident.

"How do we become one of them?"

"Period." Meme smacks her lips.

We follow behind them in safe distance. We march for miles demanding justice for George Floyd and equality.

The group thins once the black militia leaves. We're all just standing around recapping the progress we pray we make during our protest today.

KSSSHHH!!!

Everyone ducks at the sound of shattering glass.

Out of nowhere, a crowd of people rush through the streets of downtown Houston.

Trashcans and crowbars are used to break into high-end stores in the area.

Meme's chest rises and falls with rapid breaths.

"It's okay. I got you." I grab her hand.

"Let's get out of here."

"Pria." I whip my head around so fast when I hear Pierre's voice.

"AAAAHHHH!"

"Yeah, nigga! You think you gon' screw my sister and friend and get away with it?"

I press the taser against his flesh on full power.

I watch his body jump around like a fish on dry land.

"That's enough." Meme grabs my wrist when she notices him foaming at the mouth.

"You waste of flesh!" I scream, kicking him in the stomach.

"UGGHHH," he chokes.

My kick to his stomach sent him into a coughing fit.

"I'm…I'm…"

"Don't even try it." I stomp back over to him.

"Pria, let's go! I know you hear those sirens coming! They're going to think we are looting too! I'm going to the car! I suggest you be right behind me!"

I watch Pierre struggle to his feet. I can tell he's still weak from the taser. Serves him right to think that an apology will smooth over all the pain and humiliation he caused.

"I deserved that."

"I know."

"What are you doing down here? We both know you're not here to fight for the Black Lives Matter movement."

"I'll be a jack boy until the day I die."

"Yeah, like you tried to rob me?"

"I wasn't going to hurt y'all. I'm going to get back right by any means necessary. Running up in these rich stores is the way to do it. I'm about to have the entire hood in Gucci."

"You gon' run up in the wrong person store and get your cap blew back."

"I don't get shot, Pria. I do the shooting."

"Lotti though?"

"Man, I told you she wasn't your friend, but you ain't want to hear it."

"Yeah, you left out the part where you were saying that because you were smashing her behind my back."

"You might as well hear it from me. Lotti's pregnant."

ZZZZZZZZZZ!

I put my taser to his balls so fast he doesn't have time to react before I fry them jokers.

"Ooowwwweeee!!"

"Nigga stop playin' with me. That girl is paralyzed from the waist down."

"Yeah, that's what we thought. We were wrong," he pants, struggling to breathe with his hands firmly planted between his legs.

I kneel down to hover over him. "Why you telling me? We ain't together!"

"Just thought you should know. Please stop tasing me!"

"Oh, now you want to make sure I'm up to speed. Where was this conviction when you were screwing my sister and whoever else would open their legs for you? You didn't care about telling me then."

"Pria, I got so much going on I don't know what to do. Buck still got me on the line for the weight I went down with on my last bid. He wants his money plus interest. I was working and pawning stuff so I could try to get enough to reup."

"You make me sick to my stomach. If you died today, I wouldn't bat an eye."

"That's how you feel?"

"Yep."

I leave him curled up looking stupid. I feel vomit rolling around in my stomach. How could Lotti get pregnant by Pierre?

I always had hope that if he ever got it together we would be perfect. The time we spend apart haunts me. All I think of is when we finally work through all this crap and find happiness how much time we wasted.

I pull out my phone to call my sister.

"What do you want?"

"I just wanted to check on you. I know the hood clowning you."

"Clowning me for what? Don't be calling me on no B.S. Pria!"

"I'm not. I just know him getting Lotti pregnant is sending Coppertree up," I laugh before hanging up.

She immediately starts blowing up my phone but I don't bother to answer.

"Ain't no fun when the rabbit got the gun, trick." I click my tongue.

"Bout time!" Meme snaps when I finally make it to the car. "What took you so long?"

"Pierre was telling me he got my former best friend pregnant."

"Girl, I know he didn't! I mean how low can he go?"

"Apparently lower than the pits of hell."

"I'm sorry, Pria." She places her hand on mine.

"No, I needed that hurt to make this break-up real. We've never been broken up this long but it felt different this time. Pierre showed me time and time again that he doesn't care about me. I still hung on to him hoping he would see the value in me."

"You need to see the value in you. That's the only way you won't tolerate his foolishness and keep struggling with backsliding to him."

"I know. I have so much to prove to myself. I've been doing okay, but I still have some healing to do."

My mind is so toxic. I could be happy if I stop sitting around thinking about how everyone around me tried to break me.

"Are you going to answer that?"

"What?"

"Your phone is vibrating."

"Girl, I wasn't paying attention." I pull it out of my fanny pack.

It's my sister calling. I press ignore with the quickness.

I'm at my limit with the foolishness for today. Between the protesting, tasing, and arguing.

"It may be important," Meme volunteers an opinion I didn't ask for.

"She doesn't want anything. Trust me."

My phone keeps vibrating so I finally answer, "What?"

"Pierre got shot!" she screams through the phone as soon as she realizes I picked up.

"What? I just left him. How did he get shot?"

"What you mean you just left him?"

"Girl, you are so simple-minded. I saw him downtown."

"You have a new man yet?"

"Your kids know who they really daddy is yet? Tramp, how did he get shot?"

"Oh, anyways. He was trying to run up in somebody store downtown, and they weren't having it. They say he alright, but I need a ride to go check on him. Can you come pick me up?"

"Girl, if you don't get your meth-smoking, dead coochie, non-existent edge-having-"

"I know you didn't! All you had to say was no you Bitter Betty!"

"Get a ride from Lottie. Y'all the ones sharing him," I end the call.

"What happened?"

"Pierre got shot."

"Oh my God! Do you want me to take you to the hospital? They most likely took him to St. Joseph's."

"I'm not going up there. He's not my headache anymore. I'm not about to be up there about to fight them over a piece of meat they're sharing."

"If you change your mind, I will go with you. You know I would never judge you."

"I know, but I'm good."

We walk into the house and kick our shoes off at the door.

Meme go to the refrigerator and grab two bottles of water so we can rehydrate.

"I wonder what's being reported about the protest." Meme's eyebrows form an M in the middle of her forehead.

"We have breaking news here on Fox. There was an officer-involved shooting about an hour ago. The four officers haven't been identified yet, but as soon as we have that information we'll update the public. The victim is Black Lives Matter activist Malcolm Jenkins. Jenkins is known in the African American community as "The Voice". His passion for equality has landed him on several news outlets across the state. We are not sure of his condition but will update you as well as soon as we know more. As you can imagine, amid the murder of George Floyd, the city of Houston is in an outrage. The crowds have reconvened and the police are out in full riot gear. We will keep you posted as things evolve."

"Man, we left just in time." I turn to Meme in disbelief.

"I know, right? Man, this the last thing the city needs. You know they're going to tear downtown up!"

"Houston not about to play with them people."

"Do you still want to go down there in the morning?"

"Girl, I have to work, but I can meet you there when I get off. You be careful! Everyone is going to be on edge. If Malcolm doesn't make it, things could get violent down there."

"I'll be fine. I'll have my gun on me."

"Meme, that is not a good idea."

"I have my conceal and carry, and best believe Bertha gon' be on my hip! I'm not about to play with nobody down there."

"If them cops see that gun, they can use it as an excuse to shoot you!"

"No they can't. I have a right to bear arms, and that's exactly what I'm going to do!"

"I just don't want anything to happen to you. They are looking for a reason to turn the streets red with our blood, Meme. You gotta be smart right now."

"I am. That's why I'll have my tool on me."

I realize I'm not about to win this argument so I leave it alone.

"Well, be careful. I'll be there as soon as I get off."

"Okay, Pooh."

I hug her and go to my bedroom to get ready for bed.

I'm booked tomorrow.

CHAPTER THIRTEEN

EZRAH

Ivy has me driving her around as usual. The majority of the force was assigned downtown. It's been wild these few days with the protest. A lot of cops are on edge. I don't think that's a good combination when emotions are already high in the community. Some have been doing their best to deescalate situations and others are waiting for anyone to try them so they can burn them down.

"Does it bother you to get the side-eye when we're patrolling the hood?"

Ivy tosses her head from side to side as if she's bouncing the idea back and forth.

"Nope. I'm here for them whether they want me to be or not. They need our faces in the hood. Not all of our blue brothers and sisters hate the color of our skin. Some are actually cool and joined the force for the right reason."

"You know people group us all together. Even my sister and her friend treat me like an enemy."

"The lil' friend that stood you up? Didn't you learn anything from dating Alysia?"

"It's not the same thing. Capria's different."

"You always think they're different. They all gon' keep breaking your heart because you're supposed to be with me," she cracks a dry joke.

When Ivy takes those lil' jabs it makes me uncomfortable. She's my ace, but I don't look at her romantically. I keep trying to let her know, but she ignores it every time.

"Is that what it is?"

"Yep," she pops her lips.

A call came over the speaker from dispatch that someone was shot near our area.

Ivy responds letting them know we're on our way. It's so much going on between the pandemic and the recent police shootings you would think people would be in the house.

"Hey, turn off down there." Ivy stretches her arms out almost hitting me in the face. "It's a short cut."

"This not the location. It's a few blocks up," I explain to her.

"I know this hood better than you, man. I've been on this beat for over ten years. Trust me. It's a short cut."

I pull behind the other patrol car. When we walk inside, two white cops have a black man hemmed up against the wall in the house.

He stumbles into the stack of liquor-stained crates he's using as a table when the tall bald one pushes him. His face is twisted like a hooker's hard washcloth after a bird bath.

"What's going on here, Adam?"

Ivy walks up to Adam as if she knows him. I hang back by the door, but I can see everything unfolding.

My palms are sweating and the smell of beer from the old bottles submerges my nostrils.

The hum of the air conditioning above is drowning out some of what is being said.

"I ain't do nothin'!" The perp keeps pacing back and forth yelling. "You see they got me hemmed up but not telling me why they here. What probable cause do you have to be in my house? I didn't call y'all."

The man locks eyes with Ivy waiting for her to intervene on his behalf.

"Quit moving and stand still until we get this figured out. Dispatch gave us this address for a domestic dispute going on."

"Did you guys see anyone else when you got here?" Ivy asks.

"We were just about to search before you interrupted us." He narrows his eyes and squints them.

"You can't search my house! I know my rights!"

"Stay back!" Adam yells, pushing the man into the mildew and graffiti-stained walls.

The man's head bounces against the wall. The gash is spewing blood down the back of his neck.

Furious, he hurls his body at Adam.

Ivy and the other cop run up to assist him, but before they can make it, two shots ring out. Gun powder fills the air and my ears are buzzing.

"What happened?"

My baritone voice shakes them all back to reality. I think they've forgotten I'm even there. I'm new so I'm not confident yet interjecting myself into situations in the field.

They all stand around while the perp bleeds out.

"I'm going to call this in," I tell them as I reach for my radio.

"Wait," Ivy calls to me.

"Wait for what, Ivy? This man needs medical attention!"

"Is your body cam on?" She slow jogs over to me.

"No, I wasn't expecting this. I was going to turn it on when we got to where we were supposed to go. We shouldn't have been here, Ivy!"

"Well, we are! Adam, do y'all have your body cams on?"

"No, we didn't get a chance to turn ours on either."

"That's real convenient." I shake with fury. "And you sittin' here helping them?"

I get on my radio and call not only for first responders but the back-up.

"You need to think about what you're doing! You don't want to get on their bad side."

"Their bad side? I was hired to make a change and this is exactly what I want to prevent! Us getting murdered in dark allies and being painted as dangerous criminals! You ain't no better, Ivy!"

"No, I'm smart, and you better be, nigga! The Blue Bloods will either let one of these people out here kill you or make sure you get hit by friendly fire. Either way you die if they don't have your back out here," she rants through gritted teeth.

Adam and the other cop are casually tucked away in a corner near the body.

I run over to him to check his vitals. I immediately revert back to my first responder training.

He has a pulse, but it's weak.

From what I can tell, he has two entry wounds and only one exit. That means one bullet is still lodged in him somewhere.

I'm not moving him because I don't want the bullet to possibly travel.

I apply pressure and I'm relieved when the first responders show up.

They aren't my former co-workers but I'm glad to see them all the same.

They take his body away and our eyes buck when the chief storms our way with darkness flitting across his face.

"What happened here?" He forces himself to the center of our circle.

A circle I have no business being in.

My blood is boiling like acid on a piece of flesh. I get sucked in like a black hole.

The wind whines in my ears as I stand cemented in place.

Am I being punked? I have to be. There's no way this is happening to me.

"Internal affairs will be meeting will all of you first thing in the morning! I can't believe you imbeciles let this go down with all that we have going on right now. You had one job tonight! Just the one! The media is going to grind us up like cheap pork and stuff us like sausage! This better be a clean shoot. If not, the media will crucify you. For God's sake the city is in an uproar over George Floyd!"

We all stand there like we're a bunch of kids getting scolded by our father.

"Let's go," Ivy mumbles, brushing my shoulder as she storms by.

The side of Ivy I've seen tonight makes me despise her.

"I'll drive," she reaches out her hands for the keys.

I toss them to her and get in on the passenger side.

"Look, I hate how this played out, but it was bound to happen sooner than later. We in a tough position. We're black and that means we should be standing up for our people. I'm going to keep it all the way one hundred with you, you better learn to back the blue. If you're not afraid to end up like ole' boy in that house then you go ahead and be a civil rights activist. Just remember how some of their fights ended."

"I can't believe you lettin' them white folks punk you."

"You don't get to judge me. Ain't no shame in wanting to stay alive. You or nobody else gon' make me feel bad about it. We'll see how your tune change once the media get a hold of this story. Once the city brings down that pressure to reveal who's involved then we'll see who side you're on. They gon' see you as blue, not black, Ezrah."

I feel like all of the oxygen is being sucked out of that squad car like a vacuum.

I have so many mixed emotions. I know what Ivy is saying is probably true but the way she's sitting there and let that man fight for his life is more than surviving. She's right over there with them trying to get her story straight.

Ivy jams the car into park and turns to me. "I need to know what you're going to say to I.A. in the morning."

"I don't know."

I leave her sitting in the car with her thoughts. I pray worry will eat her alive tonight like a flesh eating fungus.

*   *   *

"No! No! Wait!"

I jolt out of my sleep. I'm drench in perspiration causing my bed to feel like I peed on myself. The cold air dances across my skin making goosebumps form. I shiver and quickly pull my shirt over my head.

My boxes are still scattered all over my condo. My books are stacked in the far corner.

I wish I had more time to sit and enjoy a good book but I'm always too busy to slow down.

I put on a dry shirt and go into the kitchen to get something to drink.

I rest my palms on my icy kitchen counter as Ivy's words bounce against my brain like a vicious game of dodge ball.

I joined the force to be the change not conform to the corrupt behavior that's killing the black community like a stage four cancer.

My phone dances around on the nightstand next to my bed. I pick it up and see that Capria's calling.

I'm still salty at her for not showing up, but I'm feeling her. I want to get to know her in any way that she allows me too.

"Hello." I clear my voice once I realize sleep is still sitting in my throat.

"Good morning. I'm sorry for calling you so late, but I saw on the news that four officers were involved in a shooting of another unarmed black man. Are you okay?"

"Why are you asking me that?"

"Meme told me you were on duty last night. I know we came down hard on you, but we still care about your safety. It sounded sketchy to me. Do you know anything about it?"

"You know I can't talk about anything like that even if I did. I'm okay though. Thank you for asking."

"No problem. I'm sorry about standing you up, but I had a lot going on yesterday. I know it seems like I'm flaky but I just want to make sure I'm healed before I invite anyone into my world again. You keep your head up though. The activists in the community are pressing the Houston Police Department to release the names of all the officers involved. I know things are already crazy and this is the last thing y'all need."

"You ain't never lied. Thanks for checking on me, but I have to get ready. I'm going to see my dad today."

"Okay. Stay safe."

"Thanks."

I have to get off the phone with Capria. I want to expose my soul's cry and worry to her, but I can't. Not only is it illegal, but I don't feel like I can trust her with the weight of my heart.

I pull out my phone and read the last text my mother sent to me before she passed shortly after.

"Son, I know your father is hard on you, but know that he loves you. I'm so Godly proud of you. You've had the courage to do what's in your heart and go after your dreams. I love you with everything in me. I remember like yesterday holding you in my arms at nineteen years old telling you that I would always keep you safe. You are my sonshine, and I will always be here for you no matter what. Keep being you Ezrah."

I wipe a single tear that crawls down my cheek and falls on my chest.

If she were here, she would know just what to do. She would merge the right words together to make everything all right.

I want to stop and talk to my dad before my meeting with I. A. I don't know if it will do any good because he hates police officers.

My father has always made me feel like nothing I did was good enough. I can always improve whatever I present to him.

When I became a first responder he said, "It's a lazy alternative to becoming a doctor, but at least you're working."

When I graduated from college with my Criminal Justice degree he said, "All those years in school, and that's the best you can do?"

I've never disrespected my father, but I'm desperate for his approval. I'm hungry to hear him tell me that he is proud of me. I long to hear him say that he loves me. I just want him to... see me.

It's pouring down outside so I grab my umbrella. It's still hot in Texas so the rain just makes me feel sticky.

Flying through the maze of cars, I finally arrive at my father's house. I stifle the engine's growl and fling my door open.

Hopping over the water puddle, I sprint to the front door and ring the doorbell.

I don't bother calling my dad to let him know I'm coming because he will just say something smart to make me rethink confiding in him. I really need my dad right now. I need him to remind me who I am.

"Why you knockin' on my door in this cold weather? Don't you have someone you should be harassing?"

"I'm actually off today, but I have to go in and speak with Internal Affairs."

"Internal Affairs? You ain't even been on the force a good two months. Why you already gotta speak to them?"

I sit there silent.

"Cat got your tongue? I asked you a question, boy."

"There was a shooting last night," I choke out.

"I know you ain't talkin' about that man who was shot in the crack house?"

"Yes, sir. That's the one."

"What that got to do with you? You shot him?"

"No. I was there. Two white cops pulled him over. Me and Ivy pulled in behind them. I guess Ivy thought it looked suspicious so we stopped to see what was going on. The perp was arguing back and forth with them. He said if he wasn't being charged, he should be able to leave so he tried to walk off. Him and the other cop got into a tussle and the next thing we heard was two shots. No one had their body cameras turned on."

"There's quite the ruckus going on about those body cameras not being on. They haven't released the identities of the cops, but when people find out that you and Ivy were there black, folks gon' turn on y'all like mad dogs. That's why you here?"

"Yes, sir. I don't know what to do. Ivy said if I tell the truth I will be putting a target on my back. She said they will let me die if they don't kill me themselves."

My eyes plead with my dad to understand and help me. I want him to tell me what to do. I already know, but just a few encouraging words for me will let me know I can take them on. I will boldly go against the grain.

"Don't look at me! I told you they were crooked and you still went out and joined. You had too much potential for you to settle as a paramedic and a cop. Now look at you. I don't know what to tell you. You made this bed now you gotta lie down in it and let the bed bugs eat you alive." He takes another sip of his beer.

"Is it going to kill you to show me any form of kindness or understanding?'

"I ain't raising no Pillsbury Doughboy! You want to be coddled then you need to get you a woman. You can let her breastfeed you and make you think everything is going to be alright. I'm not doing it! They just killed a black man in the middle of the street in front of people. These black folks about to tear y'all apart. You included as soon as they see your black face."

"Well, you've been a lot of help," I say sarcastically, getting up to leave.

"Next time, call before you come to my house, boy. Got my blood pressure up and I just took my medicine."

I ignore him and just leave. I don't know what makes me think he will help or even attempt to understand.

I can feel the sweat trickling down my back. I scan my badge and the door clicks to let me into the building.

I.A. is speaking to us one by one in debriefing rooms. I got here early so I go to the break room to get coffee.

The two officers from the other night are in there mumbling under their breath.

As soon as I put my money in, there's a loud explosion forcing the power in the machine to go out.

"Hey, rookie." Adam makes his way over to me.

"What do you want?"

"I just want to make sure our stories are the same."

"If you didn't do anything wrong, then why are you trying to check my story?"

"Because you're new, and you don't know how this works."

"How what works?"

"Code blue. We are brothers on the force and family sticks together. It can be lonely out there in the field if people feel like you're not family. What's that you people say? Snitches get stiches." He looks back at the other guy laughing.

I grab him by his collar and slam him against the vending machine.

"Hey, man. Chill out," he pants.

"I ain't doin' nothin'. I'm not somebody y'all can haze or bully. I will beat the racist out of you if you try me again. You better worry about me in the field. I'll lay you down and call it friendly fire, my boy."

Adam turns beet red. Once I can smell the fear on him, I let him go.

The power pops back on. I make my selection and take a seat. Adam and his partner scurry out of the break room. They better spread the word because I ain't the one.

CHAPTER FOURTEEN

CAPRIA

Ezrah is being extremely elusive on the phone. I've been keeping him at a distance but it's for his protection. I know that Pierre isn't fully out of my system so it will be unfair to bring him into such a situation. From what Meme told me, he's been through a lot. That girl Alysia was so thirsty to get with him, that she befriended Meme.

She meticulously planned every move to make Ezrah her man. She was on some Lifetime type obsession. She would pop up at his job and put an app on his phone so she could know his whereabouts twenty-four-seven.

He finally broke it off. Up until she showed up at Meme's apartment, they hadn't heard from her in months.

"Can you come with me?"

"Come with you where?" I ask Meme.

She has a worried look plastered across her face. She tosses her gaze this way and that, like she has plenty to say but is too afraid to speak them to me.

"Meme. Is everything okay?"

"I got an offer from the agency to go and clean the house the man was shot at last night."

"Isn't that still a crime scene?"

"Apparently not. Isn't it weird they want it cleaned too fast?"

"Well, it's not up to them. The family has to be the one who wants the cleaning."

"You think they paid them to rush and have this done?"

"I don't know, but it crossed my mind. What if they're trying to hide something?"

"Well, I have to go or they won't send me on any more jobs, and I need this. I need to build my experience so I can get larger paying accounts."

"Why you want me to go? I not certified to be there. I can't be getting that man blood on me. You know that house in the hood. When they showed it on the news it lowkey look like a crack house. My cousin was on crack so I know a crack house when I see one."

"You don't have to touch anything; this my first real job. The others have been people who died of natural causes so the family just want me to come in and clean and change the sheets. Stuff like that. This my first real crime scene job, and I need you."

"So, you remember the first day of class you told me you were in school for forensics?"

"Girl, I took like four classes and that's it. One semester and I knew I couldn't do it. What makes you think I can go and sit in that creepy house with you?"

"Because I need you to, best friend. Pleeeeasseee!"

I can't tell her no. Meme has bent over backwards to make sure I get on my feet.

"Okay, let me get my shoes on. This is supposed to be my off day."

"Are you going to check on Pierre later?"

"I'm not going to be a part of that circus. I'm sure he has plenty of people checking on him. That's not my problem anymore."

I sluggishly drag myself to the car. We make it there in no time. The neighbors are outside drinking and grilling.

I watch Meme get out and knock on the door. A young girl our age opens the door. She has her braids pulled up into a bun. Whoever braids her hair pulled it so tight her edges are bald.

I watch her and Meme talk. She hurries by Meme when she's done like the house is suffocating her. I wonder who she is to the man that was shot.

When I get inside the house, my mouth drops. Based on what they were saying on the news the man was shot.

All this dried up blood tells a different story. The house is hot so flies have started to feast on the mess.

My suspicions grow once I realize that I'm right. This is a crack house. So why does his family care about getting it cleaned so fast?

"Who was that to him?" I ask Meme.

"The landlord. She said she doesn't know if he has family or not. He was already behind in rent so she just wants the house cleaned so she can rent it back out."

"Wow, are you serious right now?"

"Yep. She's the one that's pushing this along so she can get some more rent money coming back in."

"I know you lyin'," I wave away a buzzing fly from my face.

"Let's get this over with. She has some people coming in after me to move all his belongings out on the curb."

"What if the man pulls through?"

"She said that man died. It just hasn't hit the news yet."

"I wonder how she found out?"

"I'm guessing with them having to gather evidence and her being the owner someone probably told her something."

"Do you believe her?"

"That's not my job. I'm here to clean and sanitize. Find you a spot to chill while I do what I came here to do."

The living room has hardwood floors so that makes things a bit easier for Meme. I watch her pull on some industrial grade cleaning gloves, another mask, goggles, and a plastic jumper.

With the Rona, we already have on masks, but she's doubled up on hers.

I can't lie, I'm on edge about being in that house with a pandemic going on. My skin crawls just thinking about what I'm possibly exposing myself, too.

"What are you over there doing?"

"This is creeping me out," I tell Meme still popping my shirt.

"Well, go sit on the porch and wait. I'm almost done anyway. Give me another forty-five minutes or so."

"Are you sure?"

"Yeah, I'm good. It's not as bad as I thought."

"Okay, I'll be right on the porch. Yell if you need me."

Today is the day my nephew died. I want to call and check on Nay Nay, but I don't feel like arguing with her. She normally would go to his grave and put fresh flowers down. One year, I found her drunk and passed out on his headstone.

I pull up my Facebook account so I can do a temperature check. I want to see where her head is.

I log into my fake page because we have each other blocked on my main page. On this page, I'm a fine nigga so I knew she would add me.

She's posting pictures of her and Pierre at the hospital.

I'm reading the comments from people I once considered friends talking about how cute they look together. Her caption reads, "Tragedy has a strange way of putting things in perspective."

She never could spell to save her life. It's burning in my soul to correct her and write 'perspective'.

There's no point of my worrying about something she isn't. Once I'm done, I'll have Meme stop me by my nephew's grave so I can put some fresh flowers down.

I know she most likely dumped my other nephews off on my mother. I'm tired of fussing about it because my mom allows it.

There's no point of me trying to be the voice of reason.

"Okay, I'll be ready once I dispose of this stuff properly."

I watch her put stuff in biohazard bags.

"Can you stop be by the store? I want to get some flowers for my nephew's grave. Today is the day he was killed."

"I'm sorry. I didn't know or I wouldn't have asked you to come."

"It's okay. I needed something to take my mind off of it."

"Is your sister doing okay?"

"I guess. She's posting pictures at the hospital with Pierre."

"If you don't mind me asking, how did he die?"

"Someone left a Snicker on the coffee table at my sister's house. He had a peanut allergy so when he ate it, his throat closed up. My sister was outside getting high, as usual. My other nephews were asleep. He died alone on the living room floor fighting for his life."

"That's enough to drive any mother over the edge. The way your sister acts makes a bit more sense now."

"It's still no excuse. I couldn't imagine losing a child. If it hurts this bad with him being my nephew, I can't imagine the torment she battles."

"Let's get you to your nephew." Meme places her hand on mine.

When we pull up, I can see balloons and flowers already on his plot.

When I get closer, I can tell they're from Nay Nay. She's already stopped by here.

"She's been here already." The cold stone chills my fingertips as I caress my nephew's engraved name.

Meme just smiles.

"Hey, nephew. Today makes two years since you've been gone. We're missing you like crazy, baby boy. You really broke a piece of us when you left here. Your mama ain't been the same, but God got her. I know you watchin' over her too. I love you forever and an eternity." I press my warm lips against my two fingers and place them over my nephew's name.

We slowly make our way back to the car.

"Do you need to stop anywhere else before we go home?"

"Girl, this day has been draining. Let's just go home." I huff.

The sun is starting to set on our long day.

A flash of movement catches my eye.

"Are you speeding?" I ask Meme.

"No, why?"

"A cop car is trailing us."

"Girl, that's probably Ezrah messing with us," she giggles, pulling to the side of the road.

We both turn to see if it's him getting out of the car but we're confused to see two white cops.

The bald one resembles an overweight Mister Clean, and the other looks like a knockoff of Bradley Cooper with his curly hair and pale skin.

"License and registration." His icy gaze stumbles across us both causing me to shudder inside.

"Why did you pull us over?" Meme demands.

He glares at her without blinking. "I won't ask you again, girl!"

"Girl?" Meme snaps.

"Oh, Lord," I whisper.

"I have a right to know what you pulled me over! I wasn't speeding or anything. I know what it is, a case of driving while black!"

He holds her gaze for a moment before looking away without a word.

"Get out the car." He yanks her door open and drags her from the car.

We unbuckled our seatbelts when they stopped us. We thought it was Ezrah, so we didn't think to record our interaction.

"You got a smart mouth just like your brother!"

He rubs Meme's face into the gravel.

"Get off of her!" I round the car, but the other cop clotheslines me.

I hit the ground so hard I feel like my back is snapped in two.

"Maybe if you're brother gets a reminder that he has something to lose he will keep his mouth closed. He needs to realize that he's a blue blood before he's a nigger," the bald one spits.

The cold cuffs cut into my skin when they slap them around my wrist.

"You can't do this! We know our rights," I spit.

WAP!

The blow to the left side of my face makes me stumble and hit the ground.

We're on a back road so there isn't a soul in sight to intervene on our behalf. We always take this shortcut when we come from Acres Home because there isn't traffic on this route.

What does he mean by Ezrah needing to keep his mouth closed?

They toss me and Meme in the patrol car. We both are short but we still have to angle our knees to the side to get comfortable.

Meme is nervously tapping her foot against the floor.

The bald cop viscously taps his fingers on the screen.

"Here, I found that one's I.D. in her wallet." The other cop hands it to him through the window.

"You had no right going through my things!" I skewer him with an unflinching look.

"Shut up before you end up being a dead corpse out here."

Meme looks me in the eyes and I look back into hers. I understand. Now was not the time to pop off. Clearly, they have a vendetta against Ezrah.

I'm praying they take us to the station or let us go.

My hopes of being let go dissipate when I see the tow truck pull in front of Meme's car.

She doesn't say a word as they hook it up.

"You ain't gon' say nothin'?" I mouth to her.

She just shakes her head no. Her silence makes me more nervous. I decide to follow suit and comply as well.

CHAPTER FIFTEEN

EZRAH

Internal Affairs thinks it will be a good idea if I take a couple of days off. I agree because I'm ready to bust some heads. I've heard about the code within the police department, but I'm not about to let nobody punk me.

I hear a light tapping on my front door. Only two people know where my new place is.

I pull the door open without checking to see who it is. "What do you want, Ivy?"

"Well, hello to you, too."

"What do you want?" My words are carefully spaced so that she understands I'm not pleased with her popping up at my house.

"I heard about what happened in the break room yesterday."

"And?"

"And I warned you! This is not a game! Everything I told you is true! Did you know they hauled her sister and her friend down to the station? Supposedly for a traffic violation and resisting arrest."

"What? Why didn't you lead with that?" I grab my keys and leave her where she stands.

"Wait! Don't go and do anything stupid!"

"No, what's stupid is them thinking they can play in my face and get away with it! So, I guess they tryna send a message that my family can be touched? Is that it? They got the right one. You know I don't fold. I want all the pressure!"

"Ezrah, wait!"

I speed out of the parking lot. My foot is smashed against the floor. My gas pedal is pressed against the metal.

The doors click when I buzz myself in the door. I go to one of the computers and log in. Just as I suspected, Adam and that flunky with him a couple of nights ago are the ones who hauled my sister and Capria in.

Anger spirals from the pit of my stomach. I silently pray that Adam won't be out on patrol.

I can feel my nostrils flaring when I storm into the break room.

"You think you're going to drag my family into this?" I slam my fist on the table.

"You're going to learn one way or the other the code around here, boy!"

"Boy?"

Before I can lean in on him, someone grabs me from behind.

"Aht. Aht. That's what they want."

I jerk my body forward to get loose, but it's no use.

"Calm down, bro. I'm not your enemy. You can't protect your family if you're suspended."

The stranger has a point.

"Alright. I'm calm," I assure him.

I turn around to see who's keeping me from jeopardizing my career.

"I'm Justin." He smiles.

Adam and his partner get up and walk out of the room.

The smirk on their face make me want to beat them within an inch of their life.

"Thanks, man. I need to go check on my sister though."

"We don't all have the same mentality that Adam and Nick do. They are tight around here, but they only try it with the rookies. Keep your head up, man."

"Thanks, bruh."

I head to booking to see if I'm able to get my sister and Capria out.

"How can I help you?"

"Cynthia, go ahead and release his sister and that girl she came in with."

"I don't know him like that." She jerks her neck around me to lock eyes with Ivy.

I'm surprised she's here because I sped all the way here.

"Yeah, but you know me like that. You know Adam and Nick brought them girls in here on some bull. Clear it out the system."

"It's not going to be that easy. He had their car towed."

"He did what?"

"Just give them the information they need to pick up the car. You know it's been done before."

Reluctantly, she does as Ivy asks her.

"This is just the beginning if he doesn't fall in line," she threatens before walking away.

"What did you say?"

"Chill," Ivy speaks through clenched teeth. "You need her to let your sister out."

"Let me tell you something, I will expose this entire force if I have to. I'm not about to let nobody intimidate me or play with my family. She can let her out or I can call my daddy down here. If he come down here you already know how he gon' get down, Ivy. You better ask Chief about my daddy. He whooped him and a few other cops back in the day. He will have news cameras here before you can say prison reform."

Ivy's standing here at a loss for words for the first time since I've known her.

"Now, you have point five seconds to release my people or it's up there." I lean in so close a curl from her wig moved.

"I've already started processing them out. It's going to be a minute, but I'm not it." Her voice shakes like a drunk going through detox.

"Thank you," I sarcastically reply.

I pull the card out the investigator from Internal Affairs gave me. I step out the backdoor to the precinct so I can place a phone call.

The only way to deal with a bully is to break them down. That's exactly what I plan on doing.

CHAPTER SIXTEEN

CAPRIA

I have to pee but there is no way I'm about to sit on a steel toilet that's connected to a sink. Then they have the nerve to have a plastic cup and a spork sitting on the ensemble. We are relieved that we're the only two in the holding cell.

Every time I hear footsteps echoing along the walkway I run to the window.

"I'm sure Ezrah will be here any second," Meme assures me.

"That's if they even tell him we're here."

I'm as hopeful as Meme.

"Why were you so calm with those cops when they were badgering us?"

I wadded up some tissue and run it under the faucet. I gently squeeze the excess water from it.

"Ouch," Meme winces as I clean her face.

"You have to use wisdom when dealing with these cops. It doesn't matter if you're right or know your rights. We were out there with them alone. They could've staged anything out there and blamed it on us. Yeah, my daddy and brother would've set it off, but it wouldn't stop us from being dead."

"I guess you're right."

"I know I'm right."

"Okay, y'all are out of here," the guard says.

We bolt by her so fast.

"Hold on. Here are your belongings and you need to sign some paperwork. I'll escort you out."

I almost walk on back of her heels trying to get up out of there.

There's no way I'm going to sleep on that painted cemented ledge.

"Thank you, Jesus!" I scream with both arms raised in the air.

"Y'all good?"

Ezrah's voice startles us from behind.

"Brother." Meme leaps into his arms.

He holds onto her tight as she erupts in tears. The entire time she was so cool, calm, and collected. Now that we're out, she can show her vulnerability, I guess.

"I'm so sorry this happened to you." He pulls me into an embrace.

It throws me because we haven't been able to get out the starting blocks to find out what is brewing between us.

I melt in his arms. It has been so long since a man made me feel like everything is going to be alright.

"Thank you. I'm okay. Your sister got banged up a little though."

"Oh, I'm going to handle that."

"What's going on, Ezrah?" Meme anchors her attention on her brother.

"Not here. Let me get you both home. I'll take you to pick up your car in the morning Meme."

We followed him to his car.

He opened the door for both of us so we could get in.

I knew now was not the time but this grown man energy was turning me on.

It wasn't fake either. You can tell this the type of man he was. I thought it was game when we went to the rodeo. I know the last thing on his mind right now was capping for me.

"I was at the scene when they killed that man in his house. The two cops that pulled y'all over tonight were there along with Ivy. The bald one is the trigger man. They're trying to pressure me into going along with the lie they told Internal Affairs. At first, I told internal affairs that it happened so fast and I was just getting up the steps when the shots went off. I told them I didn't see anything but that wasn't true. I was there for the whole thing. I assume they don't know I went along with it."

"What? I can't believe you, Ezrah! You joined to make a difference not fall in the line with the same crap that's leaving our people dead with no justice!"

"I know, Meme! I don't need you beating me over my head with it right now. I called the investigator tonight and told him I would meet with him in the morning. You know I would have myself if I compromised."

"Yeah, I know."

I was in the backseat checking my credit score. I've been so busy lately I haven't been doing it.

I had a goal to buy a house and to get my own spa spot. I didn't want either in the hood either. Well, on the border of the hood. I wanted a versatile clientele. More and more of our black women was normalizing wanting the finer things in life. They were making it okay to take time for themselves. For so long some of us believed that it was normal to allow life, family, and our careers run us down into the ground.

We are finally breaking out of the mould of making something okay just because our parents did it.

"Meme, I will be back to get you in the morning. Capria can you wait so we can talk?"

I wanted to run, to jump out the car with Meme, but my body was cemented in the seat like dead weight.

"Can you come sit up here with me?"

I did as he asked.

"I know we've had a hard time getting started but I know you know I'm crushing on you."

"I was until I found out you had a baby on the way."

"She's not pregnant. It was just another lie. Alysia deceived me from day one when she came into my life. She's the one who taught me how to spot a fraud."

"What makes you think I'm not?"

"I've watched you interact with people. I've noticed how you move. You keep to yourself and you're loyal. You have a drive to be different and you go hard for the life you know you deserve. You're the type of woman I need. I know you'll keep me grounded and never let me settle. I know at first, I didn't see why my sister liked you so much but now I do. We got off to a bad start but we worked past that I would like to think."

"Would you now?"

"Yes, I would."

"I have a lot going on right now and so do you. I can't think about a relationship right now but I'm flattered. I like you but I need to feel good about myself again first before I can think about making someone else feel that way. If it's meant to be then it will happen," I leaned in and kissed him on the cheek.

Telling Ezrah not right now was the hardest thing I had to do. It also made me realize that I was finally putting myself first.

I was maturing mentally and emotionally. It felt so good.

"Are you going to be okay going against your people on the force?"

"I don't know. I have to do what's right though. At the end of the day I can't fold on what I believe and how I was raised. If it come with a cost, I have to believe that God got me and it's going to all work out."

"Can I pray with you?"

"Girl, you gone turn me down and then pray for me? That's only gonna make me want you more lady," he licked his lips.

"Stop trying to seduce me while we about to pray to God," I nudged him.

"Okay, go ahead."

"Father, we thank you for another day. Thank you for your hand of protection. Thank you for always making a way. Thank you for strength, love, and life. Father we ask you continue to shield Ezrah from all hurt, harm, and danger. Help him to do right even when it's hard. Give him the strength to stand up for what's right. Let every liar be exposed. In Jesus' name we pray. Amen."

"Amen."

Before I could stop him Ezrah's lips enveloped my bottom lip. He allowed them to linger shortly before doing the same with my top. His tongue made wet trails over my puckered lips. As our tongues danced around I seductively got lost in the heat of his passion.

"Uht-uht," I gasped pulling away from him.

"I'm sorry. That prayer blessed my soul," he erupted in laughter.

"I'm not playing with you! That's just the devil!"

"Girl, the Holy Ghost was moving up in here."

"Nah, something was moving and it wasn't the Holy Ghost bruh! I'll see you later! Call me and let me know how it goes tomorrow."

"I will baby."

"Don't."

Even in the dark I could see his gleaming smile. One of his teeth was slightly chipped but you have to really be all in his mouth like I do in order to notice it.

Yeah, I can see Ezrah being bae.

CHAPTER SEVENTEEN

EZRAH

The table shakes from the bouncing of my leg as I wait for the Internal Affairs representative to come in and speak with me.

"Ezrah King?"

"Yes." I stand and shake the man's hand.

He is a slender white man with his brown hair parted and neatly combed to the side.

"So, you want to amend the story that you told to us?"

"Yes, I feared retaliation, so I thought it best if I said I didn't see anything."

"What made you come forward?"

"I joined the force to make a difference. I'd like to think I'm a man of integrity and honor. I allowed pressure to cloud my judgement momentarily, but I'm here to do what's right."

"I'm glad you reconsidered. Can you tell me what happened?"

"Me and my partner received a call for backup so we pulled up to the scene. Adam and his partner were already inside with the perp. The perp was pacing back and forth. He started yelling that he knows his rights. Adam told him to stay back and pushed him against the wall. The man bumped his head and lunged towards Adam. The next thing we knew, two shots went off. They claimed to be there for a domestic dispute, but there was no one else in that house."

"Adam has been under investigation. I can't go into the details of why, but we believe there's more to the reason he was there. Thank you for providing some clarity on what happened that night."

"I'm just sorry it took me so long."

"Going against those on the force is not easy. I know you're new but this is not what we're about. I'm not naive to believe that we don't have racist or crooked cops amongst us. You are proof that some of us are doing this for the right reasons."

"Thank you." I stand and shake his hand.

When I walk down the hall, I feel like all eyes are on me.

"King, come here. I need to see you in my office." The captain motions for me to follow him. "Take a seat."

I do as he asks.

"I want to commend you for what you did. It takes guts to stand up for what's right. That's what we need on the force while our city is so divided. If the communities we protect don't trust us it's a dangerous situation for everyone."

"I feel the same way."

"You came with high recommendations and it shows."

"Thank you. I plan to go far in my career and I won't get there by compromising."

"That's good to hear. You can take a few more days off and then come back ready to work."

"Can I get a new field trainer?"

"Things not working out with Ivy?"

"We've known each other from when I was a first responder. I think the conflict of interest prohibits me from learning everything I should be learning right now."

"Understandable. I'll have you reassigned before you get back."

"Thank you, sir."

I'm glad to have a few days off. I need to clear my head and let the dust settle as much as possible at work.

I press the talk button on my steering wheel when I notice a call from my dad coming through.

"Hello."

"Hey, son."

I look down at my phone to double check that it is in fact my father calling. He's not normally this pleasant when he calls.

"Hey, Dad. What's going on?"

"I just want to tell you that I'm proud of you. Your sister called me and told me how you stood up to them crooked cops. You make sure you watch your back around those snakes, son."

"I will, Dad."

"I'm not crazy about you being a cop, but I do believe you can make a change. Why don't you stop by later so I can put some steaks on the grill and enjoy a cold one?"

"I would love that, Daddy." I'm grinning from ear to ear. "What time you do you want me to come through?"

"Give me a couple of hours. I need to go to B&W Meat Market and grab us some steaks."

"Okay, I'll get the beer then."

"Boy, you know my beer has to be ice cold. I'll get the beer so I can go ahead and let it sit on ice."

"Alright. I'll see you in a few. I need to take Meme to pick up her car anyway."

"You know that girl wasn't going to wait around for you. She had me take her this morning."

"I wanted to pay for it since they were messing with her because of me."

"Yeah, I figured, but I took care of it."

"Okay, Dad. I'll see you in a bit."

"Okay," he says, disconnecting the call.

I've been waiting a long time for my dad to show me some type of acceptance.

I don't know how long it will last, but I'm glad to spend some time with him without him jumping down my throat.

While riding around, I notice a spot that will be nice for Capria's spa. That's all I hear her talk about to my sister, is getting her own spot.

When I call the number on the building, it turns out to be one of my old colleagues when I was a first responder.

"Victor." I jump out of my car and shake up with him.

"How's it been, bro? How you likin' it on the other side?"

"It's been something."

"Yeah, I saw your picture on the news with that shooting. I hope everything is everything, man."

"Yeah, it's a change I'll tell you that. More politics than I'm used to, but I'll be okay."

"When you called me about this spot I thought you were thinking about quitting already," he laughs.

"Nah, my sister friend wants to open up her own spa and I thought this would be a nice spot for her."

"Friend, huh? Is she gon' try and skip on the rent if y'all fall out?"

"Not at all. Her passion for her spa is bigger than anything else. She wouldn't let me or anyone else come between her and that."

"Well, since it's you and I owe you one for saving my life, she can move in this spot for the first year rent free. That will give her time to get on her feet and get her clientele rolling in."

"Man, it was just a dog," I start cracking up.

"I'm sure it probably had rabies. Had you not rocked him with that stick I could be limping around with one leg."

"I hear you."

"Here are the keys. After you show it to her let me know if she decides to move forward or not. I'll draw up the contract for her."

"Thanks, bro."

"No problem."

He walks back to his truck and left me standing there. I pull out my phone and called Capria.

The phone rings a few times before she picks up.

"I'm sorry for bothering you. Are you at work right now?"

"No, why? Wassup?"

"Can you meet me at this spot? My car won't start and Meme still gettin' stuff straightened out with her car."

"Okay, shoot me the location."

"Bet."

She disconnects, and I did as she asked. I dust off the old metal folding chair and take a seat while I wait for her.

The area has a lot of traffic, and from what I can tell, the strip that the space is located is clean, and I love the fact that a security guard patrols the area.

After she was robbed by Pierre, I insisted she get her conceal and carry but she refused.

I slipped her a taser in her bag before I moved out though. For now, that will have to be the compromise that we make on her protection.

After thirty minutes, Capria pulls into the parking spot next to my car.

"What are you doing in here? You ready?"

Our eyes locked and I could se the confusion in hers.

"Why are you just sitting there staring at me?" She asked.

"How would you like to use this spot for your spa?"

"I have some money, but I don't know if I'm ready for such a big commitment. Owning a business is hard."

"You would be an amazing boss. You're dedicated, passionate, and you genuinely love what you do."

"I finally got my credit store up. I don't need a broken lease from this shop messing that up if this goes belly up."

"Well, first of all you need to stop talking down on yourself. Second, I know the owner. He agreed to let you operate rent free your first year. He will draw up a contract between you both and go from there. You can ask him what the rent is because I didn't have a chance to."

"Rent free? Who would do something like that?"

"Like I said, he's a good friend. You want it or not?"

"Of course, I do! Thank you so much!" She turns toward me, her face lighting up.

"These are for you then." I hand her the keys.

"Shouldn't I wait on the lease first?"

"Are you going to tell him no?"

"Nope! An entire year gives me a chance to get everything up and running. It doesn't matter what the rent is, I will be able pay it. Why are you doing this? What I gotta do? Men don't do anything without wanting something in return."

"I don't want anything from you other than seeing you smile. I don't expect you to lay on your back just because I saw a way I could help you and did. It's some men out here that just want to see you get ahead. Some men are about putting their women in the best possible position to win."

"I'm not your woman."

"Yet..."

"Well, would you like to celebrate over dinner?" she offers.

"I would love to, but I promised my dad that I would chill with him. Are you available tomorrow? With everything going on, they gave me some time off."

"I am available. I get to plan the date this time."

"Sounds good to me. I like steak and seafood, so bring you wallet," I tease.

"Oh, I stacks the paper. I can afford a dinner," she assures me.

"Well, Ms. Malone, congratulations on the next phase of your life."

"Thank you. So I'm guessing you don't need a ride?"

"No, I'm good. It's good to know you have my back though."

"Yeah, you good people."

"Well, let me go because I have some more running to do before I meet with my dad."

"Okay, I really appreciate you for this. Now I can take the money I've been saving and buy supplies and furniture. God is so good, man!"

"Yes, he is."

Capria hugs me and jumps back into her car. I shoot Victor a text that Pria loves the spot. Once he gives me the details, I'll let her know when to meet him to sign her lease.

I'm so excited for her. She deserves the world, and I want to be the one that gives it to her.

CHAPTER EIGHTEEN

CAPRIA

The Next Day...

"Pierre, why are you calling my phone?"

I 'm not to let him ruin what has turned out to be the best day of my life.

"So, you couldn't call and check on a nigga? Your sister told me she asked you for a ride to the hospital, so I know you were aware of what went down."

"Pierre, are you high? I'm not sure if you're messing with Nay Nay or Lotti, but it's not my problem. My life is good, and I'm free of all the drama. Get off my line, chump." I end the call.

I've been running around all day trying to find the perfect outfit for tonight.

I opt for this back out leopard print number. What I love most about it other than its tight fit is it had a hoodie on it.

I pair the dress with some simple black stilettos. Meme says she could do my hair in an ole' nasty bob to complete my look.

I'm excited. This is my first time going on a real date. Pierre and I just sexed our way into a relationship. I never required him to do anything for me.

I didn't require him to respect me, mature, or build with me.

These past several months have taught me a lot about myself. Mainly, that I don't need a man. I am more than capable to stand on my own.

It has also taught me that there are good men still out here ready to love a woman of my calibre.

Not all men are intimidated by a woman with goals and ambition. Ezrah is a breath of fresh air.

If Ezrah can understand that most of my time will be dedicated to building my spa then we might can try making this official.

"Why do you look nervous already and you haven't left yet?" Meme teases me as I walk into the apartment.

"I've never been on a date, girl."

"Um, y'all went to the rodeo together."

"He said that wasn't a date. We were just trying to get to know each other."

"I guess. Well, do you want to take your shower and stuff before I do your hair?"

"Yeah, I don't want the steam to make my curls fall. Let me go and clean up and then we can do my hair."

"Let me see what you picked out."

I pull my dress out of the bag and lay it flat on the couch and sit the shoes on the floor like it's for the first day of school.

"Girl, are you trying to seduce my brother?"

"Absolutely not! I want to be sexy though."

"Well, you be that Sis. Trust me. Go hurry up and get dressed. You are cutting into my hair time now, chile."

"Okay."

I grab my robe and jump into the shower. I hit what needs to be washed and get out.

I take my time and moisturize my body with my Victoria's Secret Love Addict lotion.

I love how it smells with my body chemistry. I admire how the white toe polish pops against my brown skin.

One benefit of me working at the spa is being able to get my nails and toes done for free.

I've decided to keep working at the spa until I get my business up and running. Once I have everything together, I will put in my notice and become my own boss.

Once I'm done, I wrap my body in my black satin robe.

Meme has the bar stool already pulled out and everything in place.

We make small talk while she did my hair. It only takes her an hour and a half.

"Take a look and see if you like it." She hands me the mirror.

A tear fell from my eye and rolled down my cheek.

"What's wrong? You don't like it?"

"No, I've never looked this pretty before."

"You have natural beauty, friend. You don't have to do all this."

"Thank you, but I look really pretty. Thank you, boo!"

I jump out the chair and wrap her in my arms.

"Anything for you, Pria. Now, get that dress on before my brother gets here!"

"Okay!"

I grab my dress from the couch and sprint to my bedroom.

I wiggle in the dress. It fit like a glove once I have it all the way on.

I twirl in my full body mirror admiring my figure. My butt is poking and sitting up.

"Okay, I see yeeeww.," I bend over in the mirror.

Ezrah is going to be all over me tonight. I can feel it.

"Ezrah is here." Meme has a devious grin plastered on her face as she shoves in through the crack in my door.

"Okay, here I come. Can you bring me my heels, please?"

"Okay, I got you, boo."

Within minutes, she came back with my shoes.

I slip them on. I didn't wear make-up, but lip gloss is the play for tonight.

I press my top and bottom lip together to evenly distribute the liquid gold.

"Yep, they look kissable." I pop my lips in the mirror.

"Wow." Ezrah's penetrating gaze probes every inch of my body.

"Um, can you push your eyeballs back into your head?" Meme teases.

"Shut up." He nudges her. "Are you ready, Capria?"

"Yes, I am."

He grabs my hand and brings it to his mouth, pressing a soft kiss to my knuckles. "This will be a night you won't forget, Ms. Malone."

His eyes are a magnetic pool of desire.

He opens the door for me and waits until I'm comfortably inside before closing the door for me.

"So, where are we headed?"

"To my place."

"This is not that type of party, and I didn't get this fine just to go sit at your crib."

"If you don't like it, then we can go to the reservation I've set as a Plan B.

"Okay," I reluctantly reply.

I'm getting my hopes up that Ezrah is different. Him trying to take me to his apartment isn't the play. I have a feeling that spot he hooked me up with came with conditions.

He's in for a rude awakening though.

I haven't been to his new place. I'm pleasantly surprised once we arrived.

It's an open floor plan and his bedroom is an upstairs loft. It has a modern feel with African art as the décor option.

"Follow me," he says, heading towards what looks like an emergency exit.

"Oh, my goodness," I gasp.

"My favorite scene from the movie *Think Like A Man* is when Michael Ealy took Taraji P. Henson on the rooftop date. The plot twist is that I can actually cook too."

"Lord, I don't have time for food poisoning, man."

"Girl, please."

He escorts me over the small dinner table with a black tablecloth.

"I'll pour you a glass of champagne while I go get the food out of the warmer."

"Fancy."

"Wait until you see what I cooked for you."

Ezrah rolls out a four course meal that will put any five-star restaurant to shame.

I pray that my stomach doesn't start to stick out because this wasn't the dress for it.

"So, what do you think so far?"

"Are you kidding me?" I ask him. "This was intimate and thoughtful. I'm glad we didn't have to sit in a room full of strangers trying to learn more about one another."

"I feel the same way. I just wanted some quiet time with you. I know you probably thought I wanted something in return when I brought you here."

"No lie, I did."

"I'm getting used to proving you wrong, Pria," he chuckles.

"Well, don't get comfortable with that. I hate being wrong."

"I've watched you grow so much since you started living with my sister. I could tell you had been broken down by people around you. You kept fighting though. That's what drew me to you. You never give up."

"I don't know how to. Sometimes I feel I should, but something in me keeps pushing me forward. It can be a good and bad thing though. I've also hung onto people who didn't deserve me. I allowed people to treat me less than what I was worth. I will never allow that to happen again."

"So, you have your shop. What's next on your list of goals?"

"I finally built my credit score up to the high seven hundreds. I want to buy a house. I've been doing some research, and there's a broker here in Houston that can use my one year of business income to help qualify me for a loan."

"Girl, you are on it."

"I have to be. I have a lot to prove to myself. This nagging feeling that I deserve more won't leave me alone."

"As it shouldn't because you do."

I stand from the table and walk up to Ezrah. I make myself comfortable in his lap.

"Make love to me tonight."

Warmth spreads between my legs. I can hear his heart pounding as I finally come to a halt before him, inches from his face

"Are you sure? I don't want you to feel like you owe me anything, Capria. I mean that. I did that because I want to see you win not because I want what's between your legs. I mean, I do, but that's not all I want. I want all of you."

"Can you handle all of me?'

"I have two hands so I should be fine."

He swings me up into his arms as he makes his way up from the chair towards the door.

"Tonight, I make you mine," he pants as his lips mesh with mine.

Being his doesn't seem like a bad thing. I deserve Ezrah.

CHAPTER NINETEEN

CAPRIA

One Year Later...

The past year has flown by. If someone would've told me that my life would be this amazing, I wouldn't have believed it. Being humiliated by Pierre and my sister seems like a lifetime ago. Ezra and I are locked in. The bond we have can't be touched.

The smile on my face, I put there, but he makes sure it stays there. I don't have to worry about him cheating or disrespecting me because that's not the type of man he is.

The only thing about him being a cop is the fear in the pit of my stomach that he won't come home to me one day.

I push those thoughts from my head and just keep praying over my baby. I know God will keep him safe for me.

"Are you sure you want to do that?"

Meme wasn't as forgiving of my sister and Lotti as I am. My life is so good that hating them has no point. I decided a year ago to let the past go.

Neither one of them heffas are welcomed around my man, but I can move forward completely now.

"Yes, I'm sure. I finally got my house together, and I want to invite them both to the housewarming."

"You want to rub in their faces that you made it despite all the crap they did to you."

"I really don't. I just want peace in my life. Nay Nay is my sister, so it's time I make things right with her."

"Is she still with Pierre?"

"They actually have a baby on the way."

"Girl, shut the front door! Don't he have a baby already with your friend Lotti?"

"Girl, yes. A little girl. That's their drama, not mine. I'll call you when I come out of my sister's house."

"Okay, take your taser with you. That girl spicy."

"Girl, shut up." I laugh, ending the call.

I take a deep breath and get of my car. I don't look anything like I did almost two years ago when me and my sister fell out over Pierre.

I miss my nephews like crazy and can't wait to spoil them. Whatever baby my sister has with Pierre I will treat the same as well.

Ezrah has made it like the life I lived with Pierre never existed. Maybe things will work out differently for my sister and him.

I knock on the door.

"Come in!" my sister yells over her music.

I walk into the house to see her and Pierre sitting on the couch smoking a blunt.

"What you want?" she snaps.

"I wanted to invite you to my housewarming this Saturday."

"I ain't heard from you in almost a year and you pop up to invite me to your fake housewarming party. You so fake."

"Nay Nay, I don't want any problems. The past is the past. I've moved on and I want us to try and work things out."

"So, the fact that I'm pregnant by Pierre don't bother you?"

"No, it really doesn't, Nay. If you are happy, then I'm happy for you. I've truly moved on. I just want my sister back."

She's searching my face to see if I'm telling the truth or not.

Pierre's mouth is watering like I'm a piece of steak.

Nay moves towards me like a skinless snake on broken glass.

"We'll accept your lil' invitation. If I can find a babysitter, we'll come."

"You don't need a babysitter. I have games planned for my nephews. I've missed them."

"Okay, say less. You inviting your girl Lotti? If so, me and my man can't come."

"No, I'm not inviting her. It's a small gathering. I want you to meet my guy too. I think you'll like him, Nay." I smile.

"Oh, you tryna rub your lil' man in Pierre face?"

"My God, Nay! Please grow up. I'm happy and I'm just trying to repair our relationship. Come or don't, but I don't care." I drop the invitation on the table.

I wasn't about to deal with her foolishness.

Once I get to the bottom of the stairs, I run into Lotti. Therapy must've worked wonders for her because she's now walking with the assistance of a cane. She's using the other hand to push the baby stroller.

"Hey," she says.

"Hello, Lotti. How have you been?"

"I'm making it."

"That's good."

"How have you been?" her voice spikes upward as she struggles.

"Everything I used to dream about is happening, Lotti. I had to work hard, but it's all been worth it. I just bought a house." I smile.

"Really? So, stalking your credit like a mad woman has finally paid off, huh?"

"Yes ma'am."

"You made up with your sister?"

"We're working on it."

"Ain't it weird because she still with Pierre?"

"No weirder than when I found out you were with him. It doesn't bother me because I'm over him and I've moved on. How is it for you is the question? Y'all both share the same father to your children. Y'all linked for life."

"You know how your sister is. I guess it's my karma for how I betrayed you."

"I'm not gon' lie, a couple years ago I wanted both of y'all dragged through the hood by your braids. I honestly let all the stuff go, Lotti. I wish y'all well. I'm surrounded by people who love and are loyal to me. My spa is booming, and I finally got my name on a deed. I wouldn't be able to enjoy my wins if I were still bitter. I pray y'all find peace and everything works out. I gotta go. Take care, girl."

If feels good being the bigger person. Lotti and Nay Nay were still caught up in the same cycle. Still trying to hold on to a man who doesn't want to be kept.

I was once blind like that. I'm thankful for the final heartbreak from Pierre. It pushed me to go after everything I deserved. The more I healed the better things got for me.

I'm excited about my housewarming. Everything is being catered. I'm making money at my spa hand over fist. I'm able to save and live comfortably.

"Dang, Meme!"

I look down at my phone. She can't even wait for me to call her back!

"You are so nosey!"

"Girl, how did it go?"

"It was fine. I even ran into Lotti."

"Girrrlllll!"

"I can't believe I was so blind by what I thought was love, Meme. I realised how little I thought of myself back then. The best thing I did was move in with you when they trashed my apartment. It changed my life."

"I'm just glad to see you on the other side of pain mamas."

"Me too. I'm on my way home now to see if your brother has all the meat seasoned for tomorrow."

"Look at y'all all booed up. He's treating you okay, sis?"

"Your brother is loving me down, baby!"

"Eeeww! TMI, girl!"

"Not just like that. I mean mentally, physically, and emotionally."

"Is he moving in with you?"

"No. We're not to that point yet. It's no rush on our end. We genuinely just enjoy each other's company."

"You're gushing all through this phone. I'll meet you at your house so we can go through your checklist for tomorrow."

"Thanks, babe."

By the time I make it home, Meme hasn't arrived, but Ezrah is here. We aren't living together, but he has a key. Ezrah has proved to me that I can trust him.

"You got it smelling good in here." I sit my purse in the bar chair.

"You know I'm going to make sure you look good in front of all your people." He walks over and wraps his arms around my waist.

He plants juicy kisses on my lips.

"Alright. Don't get nothing started we can't finish. Meme is on her way to help me finish going over my list."

"Well, I'm off today, so we can warm up every room in this house."

"Just nasty."

"Only for you."

While he gets back to seasoning the meat, I go on the patio deck for one final look.

The trellis is wild but beautiful with the climbing vines that wrap themselves around it. The ground level stonework is beautiful. The previous owners had it repaired prior to moving.

I have citronella candles already placed on the tables so we will only have to light them tomorrow. I have tiki sticks too.

I've planned a whole vibe for tomorrow.

"I love it." Meme comes up behind me.

"I can't believe I own my home, Meme. I felt like I could do it, but I never saw this happening for someone like me."

"Well, it's happening, boo! Tomorrow we celebrate you!"

*   *   *

Despite the good loving that Ezrah gave me I was still restless last night. I was too excited to sleep.

"Here you are." Ezrah hands me a cup of coffee.

"How long have you been up?"

"A couple of hours. Just soaking it all in."

"Well, go soak in the tub and get dressed. I'll get the grill started, and by the time I'm done, you should be out so I can get in."

"Okay, baby. Are you okay? Why are you acting all nervous?"

"I'm not. You buggin'."

"Umph."

I decide to leave him alone and do what he recommends. One thing about having a man that treats you like a queen is that when he tells you something to do, you can do it. You know he has your best interest at heart. Now I'm not giving him wifely submission at girlfriend title, but I do respect my man.

A man has to be respected and feel needed. It feels good needing Ezrah for other things. I have my own money, home, and self-worth.

I need him to bounce ideas off of, to test new recipes on, to cuddle and watch a movie with, to discuss new business ventures, and how our stocks are doing on the market.

Being with Ezrah is a different vibe. Once I elevated within myself, I drew the right man to me.

I opt for a shower instead of a bath. I want to be ready just in case someone, like my mother, arrives early.

"I'm here!" Meme yells from the living room.

"Here I come!" I yell back.

I jump to squeeze my butt inside of my jeans. I pair it with a cute off-shoulder white shirt and my gold sandals.

I run my fingers through my bob. I'm thinking about switching up my signature style but I hate change.

"Hey, sexy." Ezrah bites down on his bottom lip.

"Aht. Aht. Go get in tub. I'll watch the meat. Is your dad still coming, baby?"

"You know he can't tell you no. He just called and said he's on his way and make sure his beer cold."

"I know. I know."

"The caterers dropped this off while you were in the shower too." Meme is peeking inside the containers.

"Okay, let's get it setup on the tables outside."

"Okay."

It doesn't take us long to set everything up. My eyes start stinging from the smoke when the wind veers it in my direction.

"Let me check this meat to make sure he not burnin' up nothin'."

The mixture of sun and shadow as the sunlight filters down through the trees around the patio is so peaceful.

I can hear the sputtering of the food on the grill after I close the lid back.

My hot tub is covered. I had it serviced so everything was in perfect working condition. It's the only spot Ezrah and I haven't made love.

People start to trickle in. I have the old school backyard jams blaring through the speakers.

Maze featuring Frankie Beverly has my mama swaying her hips. Ezrah's dad grabs her by the hand and joins her.

"Don't y'all be gettin' no ideas over there," I scold them.

They can't be trying to date and me and Ezrah already datin'. I don't know how that would work, but I don't like it.

They do look cute over there though. I don't think I've ever seen Ezrah's dad smile so hard.

"What they over there doin'?" Ezrah asks, nudging me.

"Man, I don't know." I nudge him back laughing.

"My daddy tryna get him some of what your mama throwin' in a circle."

"Stop playing with me." I punch him.

"Is she supposed to be here?" Meme whispers in my ear as Nay Nay walks through the door.

"Yeah, I told you I invited her."

"You didn't tell me she accepted."

"Because she didn't."

Nay Nay walks in hand in hand with Pierre. My sister is really pretty when she applies herself.

"Tee Tee." My nephews run up to me.

I'm so glad to see them!

"Give me kisses." I slob both down. "You are carrying that baby good, sis." I embrace her.

I can tell she's was nervous. Pierre is eyeballing Ezrah. He's standing behind me.

They crossed paths back in the day, but I'm praying things will be cool. I pray so I'm believing God will be in the mix today.

"Thank you," she says.

"Nay, this is Ezrah. Ezrah, this is my sister, Nay. You've met Pierre before."

"Nice to meet you." He reaches out his hand to Nay. "What's good, bro?" He gives Pierre dap.

"Well, the drinks are on ice and the food is almost ready. There's appetizers too."

"Can I see your house, sis?"

"Really?"

"Yeah. I'm proud of you, big sis."

"Okay. Ezrah, can you show Pierre out to the patio deck? I'll join you as soon as I'm done."

"Anything for you." He kisses me before walking off.

"This is my formal dining room. I'm still-"

"Capria. I just want to apologize to you about Pierre and how everything went down. After T.J. died, it changed me. I was too scared to tell you and Mama I was struggling mentally. I can't count how many days I wanted to kill myself after that. I stayed high just to cope. To see how you've changed your life for the better gives me hope. I ain't never been smart like you, but maybe I can change too."

"Nay, you've always been smart. You've just always feared your own power. Change starts with you doing one thing different than you normally do."

"You've changed so much, Pria. I mean in a good way. Mama said you were dating a cop. I'm glad I didn't bring my blunt in," she laughs.

"Girl!"

"I'm just saying. Now, show me the rest of this bomb house."

I walk her around the rest of the house. When we make it out to the patio, everyone is having a good time. Even Ezrah and Pierre are making conversation with one another.

I don't know how to feel about that.

Ezrah's face lights up when he sees me.

"Can I get everyone's attention!" he yells, turning down the music hooked to his phone. "Capria, can you come over here?"

"What's going on, baby?"

He walks up to me and drops to one knee.

"I know you're not!"

Tears start to pour from my eye ducts uncontrollably.

"You've been a firecracker from day one, but you're also a fighter. I've watched you claw your way to the top without taking any prisoners. You put every piece of you back together that was shattered. You never stopped believing in yourself, and you did it, baby. You went after everything you said was yours and got it. I just want to keep seeing you win. I want to keep seeing that smile. You've made me a better man. I know what real love is because of you. You're irreplaceable, baby. Will you do me the honor of being my wife?"

I'm standing here in utter shock. He wants me to be his wife.

"Yes! Yes! A million times yes!"

Everyone cheers! Meme brings out a case of champagne.

"You were in on this?" I ask her.

"You think he could do this without me? Chile, please. He was so nervous I was praying he didn't throw up on you!"

Everyone hugs me. My stomach drops when Pierre approaches me.

"I'm glad I got out the way so a real man could love you the way you deserve, Pria. I've always known you deserve better, and I'm glad you found it. Congratulations, ma. For real." He embraces me.

I thought my sister was going to trip, but she doesn't. She understands what it is.

I'm in awe of how much my life has changed in a year. I have everything I want. It's only up from here.

The End

STITCHES

Prologue

I was at the table studying when my dad walked in from his second job. We only had one bedroom so I slept on the fold away bed. I was maintaining all A's in school to ensure I got scholarships. My father Emmit was a hard-working man but he was barely putting food on the table.

I told him over and over that I could quit school and help out but he refused. My dad never finished school so his options were limited. He also refused to let my mother work outside of babysitting the neighbor's kids here and there.

I don't know if his hair was receding because of his age or stress.

He walked to the refrigerator to get a beer.

"You keeping them grades up Cliff?"

"Yes sir."

"A man is only as good as his legacy. You will never be worth anything if you don't do whatever it takes to have something. I was too nice so now I'm stuck at the bottom. You have to be willing to rob, cheat, steal or kill of necessary to not end up like me son. Never forget that."

I seared my father's words in my heart and on my mind. I promised myself I would never end up like him.

My wife won't ever have to work and my children will be taught the same mission in life. They will understand you have to secure wealth and make your imprint on this world at any cost.

Chapter 1

BRECHELLE

Three Years Earlier

I traced the frame of my body with my hands. My ombre stiletto nails glistened against my black Gucci pant suit. I turned a lot of tricks to pay for this body and medical school. I wasn't born with a silver spoon in my mouth. At least an empty spoon would make me feel like I had a meal coming. I didn't like my mama rules, so I made my own.

The way I chose to take care of myself nearly left me dead on more occasions than I can count. I started tricking young so as I got older, I pretty much had a clientele. As I learned to keep up with my appearance and processed just how much sex sells my quality of John's got better.

I was able to stack once I got from under my pimp. Being in contact with that man was like having sewage explode on you and soak your white clothes to the bone.

Phillip Price was the epitome of greed and evil. He was the aftertaste of eating something on the verge of spoiling.

I ran my fingers through my fresh sew-in as if it would help pluck the traumatic memories from my brain, but they didn't. I still looked good though.

I was finally honoring myself by doing what I love most-practicing medicine and looking like a million bucks doing it.

My skills were so dope during my residency I had tons of letters of recommendation. I was still working at the hospital, but they couldn't afford to keep me. The ultimate goal was my own practice.

"You must be new?"

I tucked a lock of my raven colored hair behind my right ear gently brushing my diamond earrings.

They were a parting gift from one of my tricks.

Once I was done paying for medical school and my surgery, I got out the game for good. I wasn't putting my medical license at risk for anyone.

The man standing in front of me was slightly taller than me but what stood out most was his lips. They were already alluring but the way he licked them made them just sinful. My thoughts had me already repenting.

"Yeah, I'm new. How can you tell?"

"You have that spark in your eye that the threat of a lawsuit hasn't extinguished yet," he laughed. "I'm Kaimen by the way."

"Brechelle."

"Dr. Brechelle. I like it," he flirted.

"Excuse me," I told him stepping a few feet away to see who was blowing up my phone.

It was Parelle. When I was out on the streets it was me and Parelle. We both had dreams of getting out of the life, but some days Gemini would beat hope out of you. That was what they called Phillip on the streets. He would do his best to knock our teeth in if we ever called him by his government name.

Gemini didn't care if he pimped men or women. It was all about making a dollar to him. I knew I had to get away when the girls started getting younger and younger.

When I got my chance to get away from him that's just what I did. I'm going to kill Tamara for giving Parelle my number. We ain't all cool like that no more.

I pressed ignore and opened my Twitter app. I slid my fingers across my keypad until my message was complete. It was only seven words, but I was about to manifest them.

"You have me feeling like a stalker," I could feel Kaimen's sweet warm breath on the side of my neck.

"I was just letting Black Twitter know that you're my future husband," I stuffed my phone back in my purse.

"Is that so?" He flashed me those pearly whites bouncing on his tiptoe.

"It is."

"Okay so future wife let's blow this joint and get some real food!"

"Yes, let's."

We took separate cars to a quaint bistro near downtown Houston. I parked my old school Mercedes next to his big body one.

I was working my butt off to slide these buns into something just like it. I got this old one because it's what I could afford right now if I wanted to ride in something foreign.

Kaimen hurried out of his car to open my door.

"You have to lift up on it as you pull it," I yelled through the window.

My face felt feverish with embarrassment but Kaimen wasn't tripping. Once he finally got the door open, I stepped out. He grabbed me by the hand and escorted me to a cozy spot on the patio.

He waived to the waitress as we passed which let me know he was a regular here.

I know he better not be bringing me somewhere he brings all his potential chicks because I'm nothing like the rest.

"So, what is your specialty?"

"Gender reconstructive surgery."

"Shut the front door! Let me lock you down before you blow up," he grabbed both sides of his head as if he couldn't believe what I just said.

"I have some offers but no one is willing to pay me what I'm worth. I'm in the process of getting published."

"Already?"

"Yep."

"That's dope! I'm just a lowly Gynecologist," he joked. "My brother is a big-time plastic surgeon."

"Oh, that's amazing! I wonder if he can point me in the right direction."

"Write down on a piece of paper what you want to make."

"Are you serious right now?" I stopped eating my salad to discern if he was playing with my emotions. "You don't even know me like that?"

"You not sounding like a future wife right now," he slid the napkin over to me.

I pulled a pen from my purse and wrote the six-figure number I knew I deserved starting out.

"You foul! You see me calling you this entire time! You could've been dead or anything. You don't even care! Yeah trick I know where you came from! Straight out the hood!"

A tingling of adrenaline started course through my body. I know this Negro didn't come down here and clown me in front of my future baby daddy. You always find Parelle in the hood talking loudly, walking fast and lying to hustle upon a dollar.

There's no way I'm going to associate myself with him anymore now that I'm on my way to living the life I've always deserved.

Parelle was openly gay but he wasn't the clean-cut kind. After Gemini cut him loose, he just started doing strange things for a little bit of change.

Gemini ran his business like DCFS. Once you aged out of the system, he didn't want anything to do with you.

I slowly started to pull away from Parelle as I progressed in medical school. For some reason he feels I owe him something.

"Do we have to do this now?" I spat.

"Evidently we do! Hey mista' sophisticated man," he snapped his mouth open and flicked his tongue mimicking Ms. Pearly, the landlord on *Friday After Next*.

"NO... WE...DON'T!" I gripped his arm like a python.

"Get yo' hands off me lil'-"

"Parelle...please," my eyes pleaded with him to stop his verbal assault and display of ghetto theatrics.

He reluctantly followed me far enough away so Kaimen couldn't hear us.

"Look, I haven't been ignoring you. The dude I'm with trying to plug me with a job at the hospital. You know I need this P."

"Look, I know you in doing your doctor thing but don't forget who was in the trenches and knows the REAL you," he stressed eyeing me from head to toe. "And stop wearing that fake designer. It looks cheap. Let me get forty-dollars," he held out his hand.

I reached in my pocket and slapped the money in his palm.

"Now can I get back to this hustle?" I tilted me head to one side toward Kaimen.

I could see him out of the corner of my eye watching intently.

"Get our money boo," he clapped his hands and walked off.

I had no idea how he even got downtown but one thing I do know about Parelle is that he gone make something shake.

I need to disappear on him ASAP! I'm changing my number as soon as I leave here and taking down all my social media accounts. If I want a fresh start, I need to get low.

It was like cement was sitting in my stomach as I sauntered back over to Kaimen.

"Kaimen I need to-"

"You don't have to explain."

"No, I need to tell you something about me. About my past. I want you to know everything about me upfront. I don't want any secrets between me and my future husband."

"I've seen all I need to see. Sometimes when you outgrow people, they don't like it. As a matter of fact, they will try to pull you back in the barrel where they feel you belong. You handled that with poise and grace. Reminds me so much of my mother in tight situations."

"Thank you."

I wanted to let my skeletons out of the closet before I fell in love with this man but he wasn't trying to hear it. If he only knew...

Chapter 2

ALLACIA

I rolled my eyes as Martine vented about her boyfriend's latest indiscretions. I've been telling her for years to stop dating black men. Dating white was the best thing to ever happen to me.

"Girl, I can't believe after Vonte dropped off that Henny lovin' last night. Man, we were going at it like savages for hours."

"You talking about that Henny lovin' lasting long. Have you ever tried pressed juice what grass shot pipe? It definitely hits different girl!"

"You know Vonte only drink Hennessey. Piss be smelling like ammonia."

"Yet you still screw him."

"I'm breaking up with him for real this time. I need to find some inner healing and get my vibrations up."

"All you need to do is leave that no good man you're trying to raise alone and you'll be alright," I badgered her. "I told you Niles has a friend that wants to meet you. Stop dumbin' yourself down and make these men come up and get it!"

"Girl, I'm all about black love and that's it. I don't have anything against those of you that have found it in other ethnicities but he would have one time to call me a nigger and I'm going to jail. Period Pooh."

"Girl, every white person ain't racist. Niles and I have had disagreements but he's never called me out of my name. You know why? Because he respects me even when he's angry."

"I guess," her response was dry and my cue to end the call. "I need to get waxed but my esthetician is always booked."

"I told you to use Nair. It's just as effective."

"Nair got chemicals in it," she snapped.

"Nair got chemicals in it but you screwing that nigga and going down on him and his mad dirty out here in these streets. On top of that you eat meat all them other processed foods so shut up! You weirdo!"

"Well, I need to get dressed so I can go surprise my man. He's been working late a lot so I need to drop off some good loving to him. I'll talk to you later."

"Okay. Talk to you later."

When the prominent Houston surgeon Niles Winchester asked for my hand in marriage, I almost took one of his eyes out trying to get that five-carat pink diamond on my finger.

He hands me over his black card without thinking twice. Once we're married in July, he's adding me on as an authorized user.

I was in medical school myself when I met him. I'm not the school type though. I'm the shopping type.

My father was livid when I quit but he'll get over it. The person that said that one apple spoils the bunch had my family in mind. Now depending on who you asked the bad apple will vary.

Personally, I feel my daddy Cliff is a bacterium filled piece of slime. He will do anything to protect his legacy. He chokes the life out of us with his demands. It's always all about the Yarbrough legacy.

I have a business degree already that allows me to do some consulting for small businesses. I help them get all their paperwork in order, guide them on how to set up their company, branding, and a ton of other stuff.

It was lucrative but not high-profile surgeon lucrative.

My brother Ario always pushed for me to pursue my singing career but that's a high industry to break into.

Ario says that one if his patient's husband is a big-time producer and she promised me a meeting with him.

Singing just wasn't my thing though. I didn't love it like that. I wanted a man to take care of me like my father has done with my mother.

I haven't needed his money since Niles started taking care of me and I was relieved. My dad complained about every dollar he handed over to me even though I deserved it.

His money was really hush money if you want to keep it all the way real.

That man has so many skeletons in his closet it would make your stomach turn if they were exposed.

I pushed my boobs up in my dressed so that my nipples were barely inside. Niles liked when I put the girls on display. He would motorboat them every chance I afforded him.

I smiled as thoughts of my baby danced in my head. Niles favored Paul Walker. After the actor's death people stopped us all the time to comment on the strikingly similar resemblance.

It was after hours but Niles was on call at the hospital tonight. I rarely popped up but I've missing him like crazy since he's been working long hours at his practice and the hospital.

I decided to head to the on-call room just in case he was taking a nap. He wasn't in the E.R. when I got in so that where I was hoping he was.

I could hear moans on the other side of the door. I was sure it wasn't Niles until I heard his voice.

"I know you're not!" I burst through the door.

They didn't even have the decency to lock it! I was mortified by what my eyes were processing.

Niles was balls deep in some Becky with blonde hair. Her ice-cold blue eyes were bucked in shock as I stood in the doorway.

"Allacia," he panted pulling the sheet around him as he jumped from the hospital bed.

"Allacia what? What do you have to say? Better yet what can you say?"

"I can explain."

"Explain screwing some chick at work? Please enlighten me."

He stood there searching for a lie.

"I'm sorry babe."

"Sorry? You sorry alright!"

I started to pull my ring off but I earned every carat.

I slammed the door behind me and headed home to pack my things. I had enough money to get my own place but tonight it would be The Four Seasons.

I don't believe in second chances. Catching Niles in that compromising position ripped my heart out but I will survive this. I hope.

I never could imagine this happening to me in a million years. Here I was thinking because he was white, he had to be right. I guess dogs came in all breeds.

Chapter 3

CLIFF

Present Day

"Mr. Yarbrough, Mr. Winston is here to see you," Esmerelda one of my staff members notified me.

"Please escort him in."

"Mr. Yarbrough I'm glad we could meet on such short notice," Kenneth extended his hand.

KSSHHH! Was the only sound being heard when the vase fell.

Kenneth strong armed me pressing my face against my mahogany wood desk. I could feel the cold pistol tip pressed firmly against the back of my head causing a shiver to run down my spine.

I was hesitant about inviting him to my home but it was the only place I was sure he wouldn't try to kill me. I didn't want people at the hospital in my business so he couldn't come there!

I was relieved I followed my first mind. It was usually right.

"What the hell is your problem?" I grumbled careful not to yell.

The last thing I needed was Darcy barging in and seeing me hemmed up against a desk.

"You know what my problem is! The money my associates have charged you to clean has been coming up short! We overlooked the few thousands here and there but now we have over a million dollars missing! We've killed people for less!"

"Look it takes money to make money! I had to open more cash businesses to clean all the money you keep laying in my lap! It's not easy! I already have the IRS sniffing around and if I go down so do y'all!"

"Is that a threat?"

"No, it's a fact! Now get your hands off me!" I snatched from his hold straightening my clothes.

I rounded my desk and took a seat as I caught my breath.

"Kenneth give me a few months and I will triple what's come up short with interest."

"If we find out you used our money for that new expansion at your fancy hospital, they will be fishing you out of the Gulf of Mexico and that's a fact!"

"Baby...Oh, I'm sorry. I didn't know you had company," my wife Darcy was right on time.

I was out of excuses for Kenneth.

"It's okay honey. We're just wrapping up. I was just walking Mr. Winston out."

His face was set like stone and I know he wasn't happy I had ended our meeting abruptly.

"Mrs. Yarbrough, it was a pleasure meeting you. Cliff I'll be in touch," he cut his eyes at me as he walked out of the door.

The freshly mowed grass tickled my nose as I slammed the door behind him.

"My love what have you gotten yourself into now?" Darcy's eyes were filled with concern.

Her black long hair was pulled back to reveal a fresh, soft face. Those fiery chestnut eyes were set elegantly in their sockets, they have watched yearningly over our family for so long. Her smooth creamy Nutella colored skin graciously compliments her eyes. She was the epitome of what aging with grace looks like.

My bald scalp prickled with shame. I didn't know she heard what was transpiring on the other side of the door.

"Nothing that I can't handle baby."

"This hospital is not worth your life! Why can't you just trust what you've built?"

"Because what I've built cost money if we want to remain the top hospital in the Houston area. It's costing one point five million per bed to build in the annex. The five-hundred thirty-two beds in the original building cost eight hundred million total. That's not including the other buildings in the metroplex. We receive grants for being a teaching hospital but it barely covers a portion of our cutting-edge technology and equipment we use. I'm just trying to build something that will outlast me."

"But at what cost Clifford?"

"Dinner is ready," Esmerelda interrupted my response.

"Thank you. Have the kids arrived yet?"

"Yes ma'am. They are seated and waiting."

"Thank you," she told Esmerelda. "Cliff please try to be more supportive of them. Every week is seeming you are badgering them for something or other. I want these dinners so that we stay in touch with one another with our busy schedules."

"Yes dear. I will try. I need to make a quick call and I will be right there."

Support is not what these kids need. They need me strong arming them so they don't lose sight of my vision.

I often tell Darcy what she needs to hear. It has kept the peace in our marriage for over thirty-five years.

I pulled out my phone and scrolled until I found Tish's number. She has been the perfect escape for me the past year.

The love I have for her is different than the love I have with my wife.

I burn with passion for this woman. I crave her and there's nothing I wouldn't do for her.

She doesn't make things difficult and she stays in her lane.

Not once has she ever given me an ultimatum. That's what makes me spoil her.

"Hello," Tish cooed on the other end.

"Hey baby girl."

"Hey daddy. How was your day?"

"It was okay. I just wanted to hear your voice before I sit down for dinner. Be ready tomorrow because I'm taking you shopping."

"Awwee, thanks! I can't wait to thank you properly," she enticed me.

Her words were wrapping themselves around my heart and groin.

Darcy poked her head in the door again signaling for me to come on.

"Okay, well I will touch base with you later," I ended the call.

Tish knew when I ended calls that way that someone was around that I couldn't speak freely in front of.

My wife placed her hand in mine as I emerged from my office.

We made our way down the hallway to the dinner table.

"Glad you all could make it," Darcy greeted our children.

"Anything for you mama," Kaimen said.

He was our most well-rounded child. He was the blueprint for all my blood, sweat and tears over the years. Kaimen was the one who really got the just of what I was building. If he continued on this path, he would definitely be my successor.

"You are always sucking up. I guess you have to since you punked out and became a gynecologist. We all know you fold under pressure so it makes sense," Ario teased.

"Yet you still manage to run around with my sloppy seconds," he shot back.

I knew the young lady at the dinner table looked familiar. Ario knows these dinners are for family but leave it up to him to ignore the rules.

"Sloppy?" The young lady scoffed.

Brechelle was clearly irritated by the petty exchange of Kaimen's ex-girlfriend.

Ario was the best and worst parts of me. He was more arrogant than I ever remember being but he was justified. He's one of the most sought-after plastic surgeons in the country. He's made millions by doing what others say couldn't be done. I made him insure his hands for over a million dollars each and their worth every penny.

"Leave him be," I demanded Ario who returned my request with an eye roll. "Where is Allacia? She has no reason to be late being that she has no job!" I asked my kids who had bothered to respect me and their mother's time.

"I think she had some kind of an appointment," Ario attempted to lie to cover for her. Those two are thick as thieves.

No sooner than I had completed my sentence she came waltzing in the room.

"Hey y'all," she dryly said taking her seat.

"Don't come in here late and have the nerve to have an attitude lil' girl!" I snapped.

Her icy gaze stumbled upon me. I could tell she was biting the inside of her cheek.

"Ain't nobody got no attitude daddy! I just had a bad day!"

"The way you talk you would swear I didn't shovel out thousands of dollars on your education. Including the medical school, I pulled strings to get you in just for you to drop out and live off me and your mother!"

"Here you go! Then you wonder why I don't come around that often," she rolled her eyes.

"Watch how you talk to my daddy," Kaimen chimed in. His wife Brechelle touched his hand signaling for him to stay out of it but he ignored her.

"You know better than to say anything to me you slithering snake!" She spat at Kaimen. "Mama and daddy think you so perfect but I know who you really are!"

I could see Allacia's body lock up with rage as she gripped the dinner knife.

"Snake? Girl, you're as useless as they come! Running around here living off mama and daddy money because you too lazy to work. Matter of fact you don't do anything but lay on your back! You need to beg Niles to take you back. Oh, that's right he went off and married that white chick from work."

"Watch your mouth before I run in yours," Ario stood to challenge Kaimen.
"You wouldn't dare risk damaging those mediocre hands," he laughed.

"Mediocre? Ask your wife how mediocre I am!" Ario took a step forward in Kaimen's direction.

"Don't put me in y'all mess! Ario how dare you imply anything other than us working together!" Brechelle defended her honor.

Those two were always lurking in a dark corner somewhere but that wasn't my business.

"Stop it! All of you just stop it!" Darcy intervened as she always did when we're together. "We're family! I don't care who shot John but y'all need to fix this! Your father and I won't be around forever and all you will have is each other! Stop this foolishness! Excuse me," my wife folded her napkin on the table and walked away.

"Look at what you've done! You upset your mother," I stood to go after her.

"Daddy," Allacia caught me halfway down the hall.

"What Alli?"

"My credit cards didn't work today," she whined.

"Yes, because I cut you off! You need to get a job! I'm not going to keep enabling you to squander your life away!"

"We both know why you're enabling me daddy! Should I march down this hallway and tell mama why?" She threatened.

WAP!

My hand came down across her left cheek as rage swept over me. I've never laid a hand on her before today but she's taking things too far.

"Don't you ever threaten me! You being cut off from my money will be the least of your worries! Now get out of my face!"

I left Allacia standing there holding her face in utter shock. I could see her body crumpling in on itself.

When I made it to the bedroom my wife was sitting at her vanity with her hand against her breastbone in tears.

"Baby, those kids always argue," I consoled her. "You know you can't afford to get worked up."

"I just wanted today to be the day we told them about my heart," the tears flowed from her eyes making me feel inadequate.

I was the only surgeon who specialized in heart and kidney issues but couldn't figure out a way to save my wife.

"I told you I will figure out a way to save you! You just must hang in there. I've created cutting edge procedures that have changed the face of medicine. I know I can save you!"

"Maybe God doesn't want you to save me."

"In that operating room I am god Darcy!"

"Watch your mouth. Pride goes before destruction and a haughty spirit before a fall. That's scripture."

I rolled my eyes at her.

"Are you coming back down for dinner?"

"I'm not hungry. I'm tired. I just want to lay down for a bit."

I kissed her forehead and helped her to bed.

We have been keeping her illness from the children. They are aware of her previous surgeries to repair her heart valve but they don't know their mother is dying.

Because of the conflict of interest, I couldn't operate on her. I'm sure if I had she wouldn't be suffering from advanced heart failure now.

After the repair, the muscles around the valve became too weak preventing the valve from closing tightly.

The only course of action I could convince her to take was getting on the donor list.

She's refusing any high-risk procedures to save her life. She doesn't want to risk having more time taken from her.

She's decided to just spend as much time as she has with me and the kids. It's the reason she started the weekly dinners together.

They think it's just their mom being mom but they don't know that her days are growing shorter and shorter.

Chapter 3

DARCY

I was in turmoil on the inside. I clasped my hands together to stop them from shaking. I could feel time slipping away from me. My family was in shambles.

I know Cliff was on the phone with that Tisha woman. I've known about her for a while now.

I've been so sick I haven't been able to fulfill my wifely duties.

I was hoping she will be able to provide him some comfort after I'm gone.

Now back in the day I would've taken him for everything that wasn't nailed to the floor or bust his head open to the white meat.

Cliff knows I don't play. I remember back in college I found him sitting in the car with Bertha Reynolds.

I was a fool back in the day. I was classy but I didn't play at all.

I pulled up on them and hopped out the car.

"So, this is what you're doing?" I asked Cliff.

He was so shocked his mouth was just hanging open. I'm not sure if it was because I jumped out on him or because I had my forty-four pointed in his face.

"We weren't doing nothing Darcy," she interjected which pulled my venomous glare her way.

"Who asked you?" I snapped rounding the truck.

I pulled her door open and snatched the bottle of liquor sitting between her thighs.

KSSHH!

"Stay out of my business and out of this truck!"

"Get her off me Cliff!"

I was doing my best to rip her apart.

Now if she had kept her mouth closed, I wouldn't have put my hands on her. She was going to have to find another ride but my quarrel was with my man not her.

I chuckled as I thought about how crazy I use to act back in the day.

Death had a way of putting things in perspective.

Cliff is accustomed to being in control of everything. He can't control my heart failure so it's tormenting him.

Both of my boys are clawing to sit on their dad's throne.

Ario has so much bitterness inside and that's my fault. Cliff was always so hard on him because he acted just like him but I started to intervene.

The beatings were getting to be to brutal and he wasn't going to keep punishing my baby that way.

I feel like I failed Ario. We made a lot of mistakes as parents when we were young.

Kaimen is a perfectionist but he doesn't have what it takes to run a hospital. I love him and he's the fixer of the family but he's not strong enough to wield the power it takes to run that hospital.

My baby Allacia is just lost. I've been trying for years to get her to open up to me about what's pushing her over the edge.

After her breakup with Niles she just spiraled more out of control. Her hope of love got buried when that relationship ended.

I'm afraid I'll die without ever knowing the root of her pain.

Chapter 4

BRECHELLE

"Baby these dinners with your family are getting wilder and wilder. Yesterday was crazy! I can't believe he showed up with your ex. That was just tacky. Then he tried to throw me in the middle of that mess!"

"Don't worry about it baby. What's understood need not be explained. Ario is toxic. Always has been always will be. He hides behind his credentials but it's apparent he's still that insecure boy I grew up with."

"Enough of that. How about you give me something to make me a little lighter on my feet before I go into the office?" I slid my tongue across his neck stopping to nibble on his earlobe.

"Babe, you know I have to meet with my dad before I go in. I can't be late or he won't put me on his calendar the rest of the month."

"Geez Kaimen! I have needs too! I swear that man controls y'all every move!"

"Watch it," he warned me.

"I'm just saying babe," I whined.

It wasn't like he had far to go. We all live on what his dad calls the 'Yarbrough Estates' except for Allacia, the rebel.

We have huge houses spaced out over the hundred and fifty acres of land. It's giving cult vibes for sure if he were to add mandatory bible study around this hell hole.

"After work I will do whatever you want. I promise," he kissed me while stopping to pay extra attention to my bottom lip. "Bre."

"Yes," I panted hoping he would negate his meeting with his father to take me up on my offer.

"You have until the end of the week to find an infertility specialist. I'm ready to start a family with you. I've been patient enough. Make it happen or I will," he said getting up from the bed.

I watched his perfectly sculpted body pass in front of me as he headed to the bathroom to shower. Kaimen was a tall cup of chocolate milk that I loved to indulge in. His fade was just as perfectly manicured as his nails. He manscaped but not enough so that it's creepy to look at when you're down there.

When I met him at a medical convention three years ago, I knew he was the one. What I didn't know is how hands on his father was. It's his way or the highway around here.

I'm just playing my part until I can get my husband from under him so we can start our own practice. He just needs to understand that it's okay to have your own dreams and build your own legacy.

Right now, I had to figure out how to give him a baby.

I ran my finger though my messy but perfect hair. My hydrated Brazilian bundles were accented with blonde highlights. I pulled the sheets from my body as I decided to get my day started.

I stood in the full body mirror admiring my physique. I was flawless. My size twenty-six waist gave way to a thirty-six-inch hips. I had all my work done before Kaimen but if I needed anything touched up, I know I could count on Ario to get me right.

Kaimen has been pressing me for months about having a child. I know I can't have kids but I never told Kaimen. I was scared he wouldn't marry me or love me the same if he knew my truth.

I decided to go through the infertility treatment but on my own terms. I had to control the narrative. It was the only way my marriage would survive.

"I'll check in with you for lunch," Kaimen said kissing me as he left to meet his dad before work.

"Okay babe."

I walked to the closet and pulled out a black plunge line Dolce and Gabbana dress and paired it with my choca leather black Christian Louboutin stilletos.

Something simple but sexy. I dealt with a clientele that would notice such things.

The six figures I wrote on that napkin when I first met Kaimen paled in comparison to the seven figures I was bringing in now.

I specialize in reconstructive surgery with a concentration in gender reassignment. I only came onboard at Lakewood Hospital Center because it allowed for an even larger bag to be checked. Let's just keep it all the way funky... I loved seeing the commas in my bank account.

Gender reassignment has always been a passion of mine but it didn't hurt that it was a very lucrative field.

I gave myself a look over in the mirror and headed out to complete my own task for the day. I pulled out my phone to call my bestie Tamara.

Breaking free from Parelle was like scrubbing funk from your body that's not yours.

I've had some work done to my face so I look nothing like I did years ago. I could walk past him and he wouldn't even know it was me.

Me and Tamara stayed connected because we have a different type of bond. It's rare and I cherish it.

"Tamara, I need you to meet me at the address I'm about to text you."

"Girl, how you didn't know I had something to do today?"

"Because you never have anything to do. Get your butt up and meet me. I need your opinion on something."

"Alright. I'll meet you there."

I jumped in my Mercedes-Benz A class and merged onto Interstate 45. I popped me a Xanax just so I could deal with these fools in morning traffic. By the time I get done with my errands I will be on top of my game to operate today.

I cut down a couple of side streets before I had to commit a homicide on this freeway. When I pulled up Tamara was already waiting for me.

"Girl why you got me sitting outside this empty building like a crackhead? Some old white lady came out here asking if I was you."

"Girl, shut up and get out of the car."

"What are we doing at this fancy office building?"

"Would you stop asking questions? Dang!"

"Mrs. Yarbrough?"

"Yes, thank you so much for meeting with me," I extended my hand to the realtor's.

"That's the white lady I was telling you about," Tamara's attempt to whisper failed terribly.

The realtor cut her eyes but didn't say anything. I was so embarrassed. Tamara was the only friend I had from my past. I knew I could trust her with my life and I always ran things by her. Ghetto and all.

"This will be your office. As you can see you have six patient rooms and a reception desk. The building and office are already wired and connected with cable and Wi-Fi. If you need a vendor for medical and computer equipment, I can give you a card to put in an order. Here are the documents if you would like to take them to have your attorney view them, you're more than welcome to do that."

"That won't be necessary. Where should I sign?"

"Here, here and here," she pointed to the pages that were flagged with red arrows.

My heart dropped at the thought of what I was about to do but I was willing to do whatever it took not to lose Kaimen.

"Thank you, Mrs. Yarbrough. Here are your keys. If you have any questions or concern you have my number. Call me for anything. I mean it."

"Thank you and I will."

Once she was out of sight, I turned to Tamara to bear my soul.

"Okay, spill it slut," she said. "You know you not about to leave your people practice, so what's up with this new building?

"Well, Kaimen has been pressuring me to have a baby."

"Well, we both know that's not possible, so what's the tea sis?"

"I'm going to set-up a fake fertility clinic. I helped a friend a while back in college who has reluctantly agreed to help me pull this off."

"You've always been crazy and known to make a way out of no way but this is going too far Bre! Now you are playing with someone's emotions. That can get you killed!"

"Look, I'll just pretend to go through the treatments. I have access to patient records; all I have to do is put my name on someone that's infertile complete with labs and voila!" I forced a crooked smile but Tamara didn't return the gesture.

"I wouldn't be a real friend if I didn't tell you that you're messing up. This is too much! Kaimen is an OB/GYN! Did you think of that? Matter of fact, he handles high-risk cases! How you gone explain some doctor coming out of the wood works to treat you?"

"You let me worry about that. Look I have to get to the office," I pulled Tamara into an embrace and locked up my new office. I had a few weeks max to turn this office into a full-blown practice.

As soon as I got into my car, I looked down to see an unknown number lighting up my screen.

This wasn't uncommon. Some of my clients had two or three phones and depending on what they needed, they utilized them all.

"This is Dr. Yarbrough," I spoke into my phone.

"Ohhh, you sound so professional," the voice on the other end caused my stomach to immediately turn.

I forced the vomit that came rushing up my esophagus causing it to tighten back down.

"How...how...did you get this number?"

"Don't worry about all of that. A better question is do your husband know about your past? Does he know how you really paid your way through school? Who you really are?"

I disconnected the call. My hands were trembling so bad I couldn't start my car. Tears stung my eyelids as my stomach bound itself in knots.

I closed my hands to form a tight fist and commenced to striking myself in the face repeatedly.

It was just something that I did from time to time when I was triggered.

How did Gemini find me?

I looked down at my phone again and the same number popped up.

"Hell....hello."

"Hang up on me again and I'm going to send these pictures to everyone in your family!"

The notification on my phone prompted me to check my messages.

I was mortified. Pictures of a person who no longer existed was plastered across my screen. I was so lost back then just finding my way. I was willing to do whatever it took to get through medical school.

I barely had a place to lay my head but I never missed a day of school. I was determined to get out of the hood and live the life I was built for.

Here comes Gemini trying to pull me back.

"You have two weeks to get me one-hundred thousand dollars," he demanded.

"I can't get that much money together in that amount of time! Are you crazy?"

"Well, you in that rich family of doctors living on that nice estate. I'm sure you can think of something," his laughed caused me to cringe.

"Okay, I'll get you the money but this is it! I want you out of my life!"

"It ain't it until I say so! Don't forget who you talking to!"

Gemini's rage echoed through the phone reminding me of the many beat downs I suffered at his hands.

I never came up short or left a trick unhappy but he still found an excuse to beat me.

I think he hated me most because I had to courage to live a life, he was afraid to.

I had to figure out a way to get rid of him. The more I tried to escape my past the more it kept popping up to gut punch me.

I was already stressed about this baby thing with Kaimen not this just adds more fuel to the fire.

I took the small glass tube with the black top from my purse.

I sprinkled the white powder on the cusp of my hand and inhaled.

When I exhaled, I could feel my body numbing all my problems.

I know it was only a temporary fix but I had to do what I needed to push forward.

So, cocaine it was.

I slid my tongue across my hand and tossed my head back on the headrest.

I was petrified of Gemini. Not just for what he could do to me but how he could expose me and ruin everything I worked so hard to achieve.

I couldn't believe this is happening.

Read more here:

https://read.amazon.com/kp/embed?asin=B08MD
HL3H1&preview=newtab&linkCode=kpe&ref_=c
m_sw_r_kb_dp_bECTFb2Z19PXV